Dear Yvette

2/17

ALSO BY NI-NI SIMONE

The Ni-Ni Girl Chronicles
Shortie Like Mine
If I Was Your Girl
A Girl Like Me
Teenage Love Affair
Upgrade U
No Boyz Allowed
True Story

Hollywood High series (with Amir Abrams)
Hollywood High
Get Ready for War
Put Your Diamonds Up
Lights, Love & Lip Gloss
Heels, Heartache & Headlines

The Throwback Diaries
Down by Law
Dear Yvette

Published by Kensington Publishing Corp.

Dear Yvette

NI-NI SIMONE

KENSINGTON PUBLISHING CORP.
www.kensingtonbooks.com

DAFINA BOOKS are published by

Kensington Publishing Corp.
119 West 40th Street
New York, NY 10018

All Kensington titles, imprints, and distributed lines are available at special quantity discounts for bulk purchases for sales promotion, premiums, fund-raising, and educational or institutional use.

Special book excerpts or customized printings can also be created to fit specific needs. For details, write or phone the office of the Kensington Sales Manager: Kensington Publishing Corp., 119 West 40th Street, New York, NY 10018. Attn. Sales Department. Phone: 1-800-221-2647.

Dafina and the Dafina logo Reg. U.S. Pat. & TM Off.

ISBN-13: 978-0-7582-8776-2
ISBN-10: 0-7582-8776-3
First Kensington Trade Paperback Printing: December 2016

eISBN-13: 978-0-7582-8777-9
eISBN-10: 0-7582-8777-1
First Kensington Electronic Edition: December 2016

10 9 8 7 6 5 4 3 2 1

Printed in the United States of America

*Dedicated
to the Yvettes of the world.*

Acknowledgments

Thanking the Creator for the gift of storytelling and the outlet to express it.

Everyone who has ever supported me in my career: thank you, thank you, thank you!

To my husband for the early morning and late night reading sessions!

Sara Camilli, you are truly a gem! Thank you for your hard work and dedication.

Selena James, thank you for your patience and your continued support.

The Kensington family, thank you all for everything. I truly appreciate each and every one of you for all that you do.

The bookstores, book clubs, schools, librarians, and social media outlets: thank you for your support!

And saving the best for last: the fans! I have the absolute best fans in the world! Thank you so much for continuing to read my stories, thank you for your emails, and most of all thank you for your words of encouragement, they mean the world!

Please email me at ninisimone@yahoo.com and let me know what you think!

One Love,
Ni-Ni Simone

Let's go back in time...
waaaay back...

Brick City, May 1989

No iPhones.

No iPods.

No CDs.

No Internet.

Pimps had brick phones.

Drug dealers had beepers.

The bigger your radio, the more respect you got.

Rap battles and mixed tapes regulated if you had the juice, or not.

Top rockin' it, windmills, and beatboxin' electrified the cardboard and the concrete.

Beat bitters and dope style takers were straight suckers.

Hip-hop was real.

Kool DJ Red Alert was on the attack, and Mr. Magic couldn't make him disappear.

Fab 5 Freddy was the underground mayor.

Jesse Jackson had hope and was so dope that he wanted to be president...twice.

Don Cornelius had *soooooooooul*.

Ronald Reagan crowned the welfare queen, while his wife, Nancy, wanted the subjects to "Just say no."

Crack was on a mission.

AIDS was dissin' and dismissin'.

And yo rep was everything. Period.

Dear
Yvette

1

Y'all Ready for This...

Let's be clear: I'm not no snitch.
I ain't no chicken-head neither.

Yeah, I got high. A couple of times. Offa weed.

But e'rybody smoke weed.

Includin' my cousin, Isis, and my ex-homegirls, Cali and Munch, who been out here draggin' my name.

And maybe I popped a pill here and there. Or sometimes laced my weed wit' some coke.

But so what?

And ok...yeah, I hit the pipe. Once. Okay, twice. Maybe three times wit' my daughter's father, Flip. Mainly 'cause he was doin' it and I needed somethin' to clear my mind. And Flip was always chilled, so smokin' rocks wit' him seemed like a good idea. Plus, he swore it would take the edge off.

It didn't.

It made me feel sick. Twisted. Paranoid. Scared the cops was always lookin' for me.

So I stopped.

I had to. 'Cause I wasn't about to be nobody's junkie. Turnin' tricks. Or holdin' down no pimp. Now *that* woulda made me a chicken-head.

All I wanted was to get my buzz on.

There's a difference.

Anyway, that was then and this is now.

Now I got a daughter to take care of.

Somebody who loves and looks up to me.

There's only one problem though.

My rep is ruined and thanks to my old crew who turned on me, e'rybody lookin' at me like I'm some crack whore, wit' ashy lips, beggin' for money, and wildin' out in these streets.

Lies.

All lies.

I barely leave Douglas Gardens, better known as Da Bricks, the complex where I live, in apartment 484.

Twenty L-shaped, seven-story buildings that take up four blocks. All connected by a slab of cracked concrete—dubbed as "the courtyard." And a scared security guard, who stays tucked away in a locked, bulletproof booth that sits behind the black-iron entrance.

To the right of the gate is a basketball hoop. No net. Just a rim. To the left is a row of twenty rusted poles, where clothes-lines used to be. It is always somebody movin' out and a squatter movin' in.

Old ladies stay preachin' out the windows one day and cussin' out anybody breathin' the next.

Winos stay complainin' about yesterday, e'ryday.

Ballers stay servin'.

Then there is me and my two-year-old baby girl, Kamari,

usually in the middle of the courtyard, chillin' on the park bench, and mindin' our bissness.

Sometimes I'm sippin' on a forty.

And sometimes I'm not.

Sometimes, I take a long and thoughtful pull offa loosie.

And sometimes I don't.

Depends on how I feel.

But still.

I'm not sellin' pipe dreams and droppin' dimes to pigs.

I'm too busy tryna decide my next move. Like how I'm gon' get a job. Raise up outta Newark, New Jersey, and finally live.

Yeah, I am only sixteen, five feet tall, and a hundred and ten pounds. Smaller than most girls my age, but I am grown. I ain't no punk. And I ain't gon' let nobody play me for one.

Family or no family.

Friend or no friend.

My rep is not a game.

That's why, when my ex, Flip, spotted me earlier this evenin', on the corner of Muhammad Ali and Irvin Turner Boulevard, comin' out the bodega, I couldn't believe it. The last time I'd seen Flip was a year ago, right before he got locked up over jailbait. Flip was thirty, and the broad was fourteen, same age I was when I got pregnant with Kamari. Only difference was the broad told on him when she had her baby. I didn't.

So anyway, about an hour ago, I'd looked Flip over in disgust, from his untamed high-top fade to his worn-out BKs. His six-foot frame was raggedy as ever, and his half-rotten mouth was loaded and leveling a buncha bull. "Heard you been out here snitchin'," he'd said.

"What?"

"You heard me." He returned my nasty look. "You used to be down. But now e'rybody say you buggin'. Guess I'ma have to watch my back fo' you drop a dime on me too."

He was tryna play me. I looked around and the block was buzzin'. The sun was fallin' and the night crawlers was makin' they way outside. People was e'rywhere. Some pouring out the bodega and some on the block just standin' around. I caught a few folks peepin' at me, like they'd heard what Flip had said and was tryna figure me out.

My grip tightened on Kamari's umbrella stroller. I needed to do somethin' to keep from stealin' on this mothersucker, so I snapped, "Word is bond..."

"A rat's word could never be bond."

My heart raced and my chest inched up from me breathin' heavy and being heated. I pointed into Flip's face. "You must be talkin' about them rattin' young cherries you bustin'. 'Cause from where I'm standin', you ain't nothin' to drop no dime on."

"Yeah, yeah. Whatever. Ain't nobody tryna hear all that. All I know is my mans told me that he messin' witcha fat homegirl."

I curled my upper lip. "Who? Munch?"

"Yeah, that's her name."

"And? So?"

"And she told him that you a rat. And the reason they got locked up was 'cause you ran to the cops shootin' off ya trap. Mad 'cause you broke."

Out of shock, I took a quick step back, then a quicker step forward. "What the...Excuse you?"

"Don't front. You know that Isis, that white girl, Cali, y'all used to hang with, and Munch all got busted for slangin' in school. And Munch said you was the one who told on 'em. And I believe it 'cause you stay in e'rybody's bidness."

"You need to . . ."

"No, what you need to do is learn how to shut up, carry yo' li'l azz in the house sometimes and keep my daughter out these streets."

I paused. I couldn't spaz on Flip 'cause I had Kamari wit' me, so I swallowed the urge to slide the blade from under my tongue and said, "Yo' daughter? Boy, please. I don't know why you worried about her being in these streets when that's all you do. Held up in some alleyway suckin' glass dicks. Or is you skin poppin' now? Yo' daughter? You better off bein' moondust than somebody's freakin' daddy. You shouldn't even wanna claim that title. Yo' daughter? Know what, let me just get away from you before I end up slicin' yo' throat for talkin' slick!"

"Whatever, Snitch. Bye."

Flip was still running his mouth and poppin' off when I walked away.

Once I got home to Da Bricks, I went straight to my room. My mind was spent and my stomach was in knots. I hated my hands was tied for the night, and it was nothin' I could do. Isis, Cali, and Munch had all moved out Da Bricks. Accordin' to Nana, Isis moved out of state with her mother, Queenie. She ain't know what happened to Cali.

But Munch.

I'd seen her from time to time, and I knew she lived somewhere around here. Plus, she still went to the same school. And one thing was for sure and two things was for certain, her lyin' behind caught the city bus to school, e'ryday.

At the same time.
E'ry mornin'.
I smiled.
Closed my eyes.
And waited.

2

Do My Thing Wit' an '89 Swing...

7:49 a.m.

I was runnin' late.

Tried to get outta here twenty minutes ago, but Nana was up surprisingly early. Usually, her midnight cocktails of Seagram's 7 and grapefruit juice had her tossin' back some serious slobs and snores until at least about eleven.

But not this mornin'.

This mornin', she was up cleanin' and hummin' gospel. So I waited for her to finish her solo and head to the bathroom, *The Watchtower* in hand. Then I knew I could leave Kamari asleep on the bed while I eased out and attended to my bissness.

Once I made it out the apartment, then past Da Bricks' security gate, I took off runnin' down Irvin Turner straight for the bus stop.

All I could think about was how Munch had me twisted.

But I was gon' straighten her out today.

First, I was gon' ask her...

Wait.

Scratch that.

I wasn't gon' ask her nothin'.

Matter fact, that was the last thing I was gon' do.

First I was gon' bank her. Then I was gon' investigate.

Munch ain't deserve to be asked no questions, 'specially since she was out here comin' for me and I ain't send for her.

Like she thought I was a joke.

I wasn't no joke.

Never have been.

By the time I reached the bus stop, the block was packed and there was a line of people waitin' to get on the bus. Some goin' to work and some goin' to school. Munch was nowhere in sight. All I could see through the bus's windows was people standin' up, 'cause all the seats looked to be taken.

Munch had to be somewhere on this bus, though; she had to be.

But.

If by chance she wasn't, then that was cool too. 'Cause then I'd just go up to the high school and rake her across the concrete in front of her li'l friends, so they could all get the message too.

I tapped my foot as I stood in line behind this freakin' lady and her stupid baby carriage. She was takin' nearly five minutes to fold it up. Finally, she made it onto the bus and bingo! There was Munch, standin' to the right of the driver, countin' out her fare.

E'rything in me wanted to hook off. But I didn't. I listened to the one thought that had told me to chill. So I stood on the bus's bottom step, stretched out my arms, blocked the doorway and said, "You called me a snitch?"

Munch turned toward me, her back now to the driver, her face to me.

The look in her dark eyes told me I'd snatched her by surprise.

She hesitated.

Swallowed.

And I could tell she was thinkin' a million things at once, none of which I had time for. So I repeated myself. "You called me a snitch?"

"You either on or off the bus?!" the driver barked.

I waved my hand, then flipped him the bird. He wasn't important.

I sank my copper brown eyes dead into Munch and said, "You got one minute to answer before I slide you across this sidewalk."

Nothin'. Not. One. Word.

"Look, young lady, you need to move!" the driver snapped.

"'Cause I'm going to be pissed off if I'm late!" came from behind me.

"That's what I'm sayin'!" came from another direction. "Folks up here have to get to work. Nobody has time for this schoolyard foolishness!"

I sucked my teeth, tuned out the static, and continued to drink Munch in. A part of me wanted to simply catch her real quick in the jaw or slap her dead in the mouth for being stupid and doggin' my name. But I couldn't do *just* that; her violation called for more.

After all, she used to be my homie.

I met her when I was ten and she was eleven. It was the

same day my mother left me, my sister, and my two brothers with Nana and took off for a neverending drug run. Munch came up to me in the courtyard and said, "Who you? You new around here 'cause I never seen you before."

I wiggled my neck. "I never seen you before either; you new around here?"

Munch shoved a hand up on her chubby hip, looked me over, and smacked her lips. "It's all good, girl. I just wanted to know who you was. My name is Grier, but e'rybody call me Munch."

I twisted my lips and tried not to laugh 'cause both them names was ugly. I failed though and a slight snicker came out. "Grier?"

"Yeah, Grier. You got a problem wit' that? I was named after my grandmother."

"Nah. I don't have a problem wit' it. It's your name, not mine. But why e'rybody call you Munch?"

"My homegirl, Isis, gave me that name 'cause I'm always munchin' on somethin'." She rattled a bag of Crunchy Cheese Doodles that she had in her hand. "Want some?"

I hesitated. "*Umm*. Yeah, I'll take a little." I held out my hand, and she poured a few into my palm.

"So what's your name?" she asked.

"Yvette. Isis is my cousin."

"Oh word? Well any cousin of Isis is automatically my homegirl." We gave each other a pound. "So welcome to Da Bricks."

After that, we became the Get Fresh clique: Me, Isis, Munch, and Cali, Munch's foster sister.

We took our first forty to the head together.

Hid out on the rooftop and hit our first blunt.

Told the same lie about sex being da bomb the first time.

Licked the bodega for jelly bracelets and candy every day after school.

Got mad at the same birds and smacked up any ho that came at us crazy.

We cried together.

Laughed together.

Swore to be best friends forever.

But then things changed.

Last year, Isis got a new boyfriend, named Fresh, who convinced her, Cali, and Munch to run weed for him in school. They asked me to slang wit' 'em too, but I told 'em no, boostin' was my thang. Shortly after that, they started chillin' without me. Movin' like I was no longer relevant. It hurt, but I tried not to sweat it. Besides, after my mother left, I was used to being alone. So I for sure wasn't about to chase no hoes and beg 'em to hang with me. Therefore, I let 'em go their way and I went mine.

At least until today.

'Cause today, somebody was gon' pay.

And since Cali and Isis was nowhere around to catch their own beatdowns, then Munch was gon' have to take this round for her crew and get tore up for the old and the new.

I guess those few minutes of me drifting into thought gave Munch some balls 'cause she said, "You lookin' real ridiculous right now. Is you high or somethin'? Asking me did I call you a snitch? And if I did, it's 'cause that what you is: a snitch!"

Wham! Was the sound of me hookin' Munch dead in the mouth, causing her bottom lip to bust open and blood to skeet e'rywhere! I gripped a scalp full of her blonde micro-braids and dragged her onto the sidewalk.

Munch's fists flew through the air like loose windmills, but mine were more controlled and deliberate than that. I swung like I was in the ring.

Two of Munch's wild fists caught me in the face. One uppercut. One bang to the left eye.

I sailed a right elbow and landed it in the center of her nose. Blood gushed from it and rained over her lips. Then I yanked her down to the ground and did all I could to stomp her guts out.

I heard her screamin'. Gurglin'. Coughin' somethin' out.

I heard the crowd buzzin', and I felt somebody tryna get in between us. I just couldn't see 'em. All I saw was me spittin' out my blade and peelin' the side of this bitch's face open.

3

Cover Girl

Noon

"*Maaaaaaa*, here she go!" was my aunt Stick's version of *hello* the moment I hit the doorway. "*Umm-hmm*, look at her. Eye all swollen. Clothes all torn up. This why the cops lookin' for her."

Cops?

My heart dropped.

My stomach bubbled.

I needed to use the toilet.

Then jump out the window.

Cops?

Stick looked at me and scrunched her upper lip. "You got too many problems. Is somethin' wrong witchu?"

Nana's wide feet slapped the living room floor with each step she took as she rushed from the kitchen towards me. She shoved a pissy and wet-eyed Kamari, who licked snot off her plump pink lips, into my arms.

Nana dusted her hands. "Let me tell yo' fast li'l behind somethin', Strumpet. I don't care where you been. But one thang you *don't do* is have the cops comin' to my door 'cause you doin' somethin' dumb out there in the street! Probably on the corner whorin' for some old man, tryna get pregnant *again*."

"Or she gettin' high, like everybody is sayin' she doin', and Scotty got her trippin'," was Stick's two cents.

Nana carried on. "Keep it up and you gon' turn into yo' mama. And I swear fo' God"—she waved a fist to the heavens—"I will put yo' ass out!"

Breathe.

Chill.

Five...

Four...

Three...

Don't say nothin'.

Just go to your room and think...

I shifted Kamari over to my left hip so I could walk to my room without her soggy Pamper pressin' into my shirt and soakin' my skin. Plus Kamari was heavy, and I wasn't about to stand here strugglin' to hold her and arguin' wit' these two, knowin' wit' Kamari in my arms I had no win if one of 'em stole on me.

I took a step toward my room, and Stick blocked my path. "I know you ain't walkin' away and Mama is still talkin' to you?! You ain't grown! You just an ingrate. Real disrespectful!"

I sucked in a breath. Pushed it out. "Move."

"And if I don't? What you gon' do, huh?" Stick took two steps closer to me. "Mess around and catch a beatdown. I ain't Munch."

I blinked. Cleared my throat. And did my best to erase the shock written on my face.

Stick bent over and locked eyes with me. She continued. "That's right. You ain't slick, and I know what your li'l snitchin' behind was out there doin'. Two minutes after you dragged Munch off the bus, people was runnin' up to me. And an hour after that, the cops was at the door."

"Whatever." I ain't know what else to say.

"Yeah, I know whatever." She stood up straight and looked over my shoulder at Nana. "Mama, I keep tellin' you, you need to stop threatenin' to put her and this baby out and just do it. That li'l money you get for them ain't even worth the aggravation."

"Don't tell me what to do, Stick," Nana replied.

"I'm just sayin'. You too busy trying to be like Jesus. Well, I got one thing to say: 'Jesus, meet Judas.'" She pointed into my face.

I wanted to slap Stick so bad my fingertips stung and my palms burned. The only thing stoppin' me was that I didn't have a pot to piss in, so I couldn't take the chance of me and my baby bein' thrown out.

I stared at Stick, my eyes lettin' her know the first opportunity I got to knock her out I was gon' go for broke.

But now was not the time.

Right now, I was tired, had a headache, and needed to catch my breath. After I'd sliced Munch's face, I'd scuffled with some man tryna hold me down. And just when I thought I couldn't escape his embrace, I managed to kick him in the sack. He jumped back, and I took off. I cut through two alleyways, a playground, jumped a fence, and ran the long way back to Da Bricks, only to find out that the cops was lookin' for me.

I just needed some peace so I could get my thoughts straight. Not deal wit' these two retards.

Especially Nana, who only cared about her liquor, her man, and Jesus. And on occasion, she cared about Stick. I guess 'cause her other five children was either in jail, strung out, or had AIDS, and she was stuck raisin' they kids.

Stick was Nana's youngest, fresh outta drug rehab, and maybe Nana saw herself in Stick.

I know I did.

They was both mean, miserable, and hated theyselves, probably just as much as I hated them.

And it didn't help any that they wasn't really my family. They was, more or less, like play cousins. My mother's boyfriend's family. Nana was really my little brothers' and sister's grandmother, and Stick was they aunt, not mine.

Who was I?

The never-ending stranger in the house.

Mother on a drug run.

Father a question mark.

Dumped in this apartment with this fake, sanctified, and nasty old woman, who didn't love me, like me, or really want me around. But she kept me here because I added $326.00 to her welfare grant.

Plain and simple.

I bum-rushed past Stick; the edge of my shoulder pushed her outta my way. A few seconds later, I heard Nana say, "Stick! Don't you touch that girl and she got that baby in her arms! And besides, I don't want no fightin' in here! Just let it go! She hardheaded. We try and tell her somethin' for her own good, and she gives us her backside to kiss. Just g'on and sit down. She ain't gon' be nothin' no way."

I didn't even turn around and acknowledge that. I just

snatched my room door open and my little cousins, brothers, and sister all tumbled to the floor from being stacked up against the door listening.

"Y'all nosey as I don't know what." I shook my head.

They all looked at me in delight before they burst into giggles and scattered into the living room.

I slammed the door behind them, laid Kamari down, and did my best to think of an escape outta here before the cops came back.

4

Lemme Hear You Say...

"Y'all know y'all violatin' me. Y'all know I have the right to remain silent," I said to the two cops, a Puerto Rican one named Officer Sanchez, who was leanin' against the door, and a black one, named Officer Thomas, sittin' on the edge of the metal table I was handcuffed to.

Officer Sanchez smirked. "We only brought you down here for questioning. You're not under arrest. When we arrest you, then you have the right to remain silent."

I sat back in my chair and refused to say another word. Maybe they would be quiet and I could get my thoughts together. Figure out how I was gon' get back to my baby. Otherwise, I was gon' lose it in here. Tears welled up. But I refused to cry. Instead, I swallowed the wet fire filling my eyes and let it ease into my chest.

I knew I shouldn't have sliced the side of Munch's face.

The moment I pushed the edge of my blade into her cheek, I knew I'd made a mistake.

I should've gutted her throat.

That woulda shut her up.

Now, I'm sittin' here, being treated like I'm Ted Bundy, the Cocaine Godmother, or some other off-the-meat-rack maniac.

Ain't nothin' crazy or outta control about me.

I'm not no criminal.

All I did was handle my bissness.

Munch knew what time it was.

She knew the rules: If thou cometh for thee, then thee cometh back, ten times harder, for thou.

It's in the Bible. The Book of Streetlations, verse 101, that starts off with "An eye for an eye."

Sooo...I don't see the problem.

It is what it is.

But all this was uncalled for—the police bustin' in Nana's door around midnight, throwin' me up against the wall in front of my baby, Nana poppin' ying-yang 'bout how she ain't sign up for this. She tired of that. How she 'bout to clean house. Kamari cryin' 'cause they carryin' me out kickin' and screamin' in handcuffs.

All 'cause Munch wanna bring the ruckus by runnin' her mouth and ruinin' my rep. But then can't take her beatdown like a woman?

Alllll of a sudden she's some soft li'l girl. I'da had more respect and understandin' if she had shown up at Nana's door for another round. Not send the pigs after me. How played is that? Actin' like she's some victim. When she's the one who did me dirty.

Gon' tell the pigs *my* name and where *me and my*

daughter lay our heads? When she know all I got *is* Kamari and all Kamari got *is* me. Yet, she gon' spit on that and come after my life? Violate *all* the codes? Disrespect e'rything?

Oh, hell no.

Now I gotta make her mama scream.

Now I gotta wash her. Completely.

"Yvette, we need to ask you some questions." Officer Sanchez interrupted my thoughts. "So tell us what happened."

I looked at him like he was stupid. "So what happened? *Psst*, please. You can't be serious. You the one who came to *my* crib, yanked *me* outta *my* bed, had *my baby* hollerin' and cryin', disturbin' *us*. And you got the balls to be askin' *me* to tell *you* what happened? You bugged out. How about this: Why don't you tell me what happened. 'Cause I *damn sure* wanna know."

Officer Sanchez snorted while Officer Thomas lit a cigarette and said, "If you wanna play games, we got all night."

I needed to get back to my baby. I didn't have another second. Let alone all night. "Whatever." I tried to swallow the lump in my throat.

"How about this?" Officer Sanchez suggested. "How about I tell you a little of what I know and you fill in the rest? Munch, your friend..."

I huffed. "That's not my friend."

He hesitated. "Okay. Your ex-friend. Well, seems she pissed you off to the point where you dragged her off the bus, in front of a busload of witnesses, and sliced her face."

"Lies."

Officer Thomas arched a brow, blew a string of smoke into the air, and then said, "Lies? Really? What part?"

"All of it. 'Cause, first of all, you see how big that girl is?" I paused and let that sink in. Then I continued, "Now how *I'ma* drag her off the bus? Second of all, I ain't slice her face."

"You admit you were at the bus stop?" Officer Sanchez jumped in, walking over toward the table.

"Yeah. And? So what? Being at the bus stop is a crime now?"

"No." He stopped walking, folded his arms, and stared at me.

I sucked my teeth. "Then whatchu bringin' it up for? Don't y'all have something else to do? Like look for rapists, killers, drug dealers? Pigs kill me. E'rywhere you don't need 'em to be. Y'all shoulda been over there in Central Park protectin' that jogger instead of comin' for me!"

"Back to the matter at hand," Officer Thomas said, flickin' cigarette ashes onto the floor. "When you dragged Munch off the bus and . . ."

"I didn't drag her big ass off the bus!"

"Then how did she end up on the ground?" Officer Sanchez asked, pacing from one side of the room to the next.

I shrugged.

He stopped pacing. "We have five witnesses, including the bus driver, who all said you did it."

"Well, if you got all them witnesses, includin' the bus driver, then what is you sweatin' me for?" I said.

"Did you slice her face?" Officer Thomas asked.

"I ain't slice nobody's face."

"We have five witnesses . . ."

"Who obviously you don't believe, because if you did, you wouldn't be grillin' me."

"We're trying to give you a chance to defend yourself," Officer Thomas said, mashin' his cigarette into an ashtray.

"No." I leaned up as far as I could. "What you doin' is tryna work my freakin' nerves. It's two o'clock in the morning. And I wanna go back home to my baby."

"Home?" Officer Thomas chuckled, leaning into my ear. "And where is home? According to your grandmother, you can't go back to her house. And that pretty little baby of yours is getting put out too."

My throat clogged up and tears kicked their way outta my eyes.

Officer Thomas stood up straight and continued. "Don't worry; while you sit in here with us, the state will find a nice little foster home for your princess." He snatched a Kleenex from his side pocket and tried to hand it to me.

I left him hangin' and pointed into his face, tears fallin'. "My baby ain't goin' to no foster home! That's my baby! And she ain't livin' wit' nobody but me."

Officer Thomas nodded. "*Mmph.* Well, young lady, with the route you seem to be taking, you're pretty much on your way to jail, and they don't have daycares in there." He got up from the table, sat down in the chair across from me, and folded his arms; his words hung in the air like a noose.

"Look, I need to get outta here." More tears fell.

"Tell us what happened and maybe we can help you get out of here. Did you and Munch have a fight?" said Officer Sanchez.

"I already told you that we did! And she deserved it 'cause she talks too much."

Officer Thomas interjected, "And you sliced her face to shut her up."

"I didn't slice her face!"

"Then where did this blade come from?" He flicked my blade on the table.

The nerves in my stomach balled up and cramps filled my belly. "Maybe that's Munch's blade or maybe it's yours. I don't know who it belongs to, but I know it don't belong to me and that's a fact. Now, from where I'm sittin', you don't have no reason to be holdin' me."

"We have plenty of reason," Officer Sanchez said. "The fight alone is enough to charge you with assault."

My heart dropped. Wasn't no way I could stay in here. "Charge me? Over a fight? This got to be a joke. You ain't never had no fight before? I mean, maybe Munch is embarrassed 'cause she caught a beatdown. But, oh well, those are the breaks. Now she'll learn to shut the hell up! But y'all wantin' to lock me up is crazy! Tryna say I yanked her off the bus. What I look like, Superfly Snuka? That girl makes two of me!"

"Did you slice her face?" Officer Thomas pressed.

"If I did, she needed it! Munch came for me. Telling people I'ma snitch. That I'm the reason they all got locked up when I ain't have nothin' to do wit' that! I got my own shit goin' on; what I need to rat on them for? Gon' ruin my rep and dog me! I can't even walk the block without e'rybody lookin' at me funny! And I should what? Just take that? Let that go? Nah. So, yeah, I beat her ass 'cause she deserved it. But y'all takin' this too far. Talkin' to me all crazy like I'm snatchin' old ladies' bags or somethin'! Now I already told you, I need to get outta here to go and get my baby!"

Officer Sanchez grimaced. "You should've thought about

your baby when you yanked your friend off the bus, beat her up, and sliced her face." He grabbed me by my shoulder and forced me to stand up, while Officer Thomas twisted my arms behind my back and said, "Yvette Simmons, you have the right to remain silent…"

5

Ain't Sayin' Nothin'...

"Simmons. Spread your fingers! More! More! More! Out like a web!" The processin' CO, Officer Washington, snatched my right hand. Then my left, pushin' each of my fingers onto an ink-soaked sponge, where black liquid rose from the holes like pus. "Don't be so stiff!" She smeared my wet fingertips across a thick white card with my name—Yvette Lavonne Simmons. Weight: One hundred, ten pounds. Height: Five feet. Charge: Assault with a deadly weapon—typed across it.

She shoved my shoulder, pushin' me in front of a black screen.

I shot her a look that straight up told her to chill.

Officer Washington smirked. "Don't even think about it." She paused, like she was givin' me a moment to heed her message. "Now hold your head up. More. More. I said *more*! What's with you?! I said hold it up! I'm warning you, don't make me tell you again!" She gripped my chin and forced my face into the position she wanted it to be, directly into the eye of the camera.

Five.

Four.

Three.

Breathe.

Then she shoved a mug shot board into my hands, with the numbers 7829013 plastered across it.

Click!

Flash!

"Now get in there and drop 'em!" She pushed me into a private room, where another CO sat in the corner next to a shelf neatly stacked with orange jumpsuits, white socks, and dark blue karate shoes.

I placed my hand up on my hip. "Don't push me again, lady. For real. You doin' a li'l too much right now. I'm not a dog."

The CO who sat in the corner stood up and said, "Officer Washington told you to drop 'em. And that's what you'd better do."

"And do it now!" Officer Washington ordered.

I sucked my teeth and twisted my neck to the left. "Yo, for real, son. Word is bond. You two need to chill."

Officer Washington pointed into my face. "Already I've had enough of you. What do you think this is, the playground? This ain't a game. Now. Take. Those. Clothes. Off."

She trippin'. I blinked in disbelief. "Oh, really. Oh, okay. How about this: Since you don't know when enough is enough, I ain't takin' nothin' off! Period."

"You will do what I tell you to do." Officer Washington gripped my shoulder.

I snatched away. "You better get your hands offa me!" I lifted my right hand to push her back, but before I could touch her, the room filled with too many COs for me to count. Then somebody wrapped an elbow around my neck, squeezed, and yanked me down to the concrete floor. My head felt like it had slammed into a pallet of bricks.

There was a pair of knees pressed into my arms, pinchin' my skin. Somebody had my legs pinned together. And Officer Washington gripped my chin, her face a breath away from mine. Her reekin' spit speckled my eyes as she said, "You'd better get this straight. I don't know who you think you are..."

I snapped, "I don't know who you think you are! But you ain't my mother!"

"You're right. I'm not your mother. Her rotten ass has been replaced. 'Cause right now, all of us in here, we're all your mother. And we're the type of mothers that don't give a damn about you."

"I don't need you to care about me! But what you better do is get your stank breath out my face." Tears pounded against the backs of my eyes and danced around the brims.

"Or what? What you gon' do, but get stomped. I bet out there on the street you thought you were bad, huh? Well, I'm here to break you, and I can promise you that you're not badder than me. And you're certainly not badder than those girls back there waiting on yo' li'l behind. They love tiny li'l thangs like you. You'll make somebody a nice wife and by the time you get finished smelling their fishy drawls, sour period, hot piss, stale shit, and anything else they feel like shoving in your pretty little face, you'll be begging for my stankin' breath to come back."

She knocked on my forehead with her knuckles. "Now,

get this through your head: This is not Burger King and you will not have it your way. You're in my house. And in here, I'm God. And God's gonna give you one last chance. Now you can make this easy or you can make it hard. Choice is yours. But if I were you, I'd get up nice and slow. And when I tell you to drop 'em, you do it. 'Cause if you don't, and you even look like you're thinking about making one crazy move, I *will* teach you what we do with nuts. The choice is yours." She cast my chin from her grip.

"I'ma get up," I said, silent tears falling from the corners of my eyes.

"You gon' drop 'em?" she asked.

I nodded.

"That's not an answer."

"Yeah," I said.

"Say *Yes, Ma'am*."

I swallowed. "Yes. Ma'am."

"That's another thing you're going to learn in here, some respect." She looked at the other officers. "Let her up."

Cautiously, they eased off of me, while clutching my arms and helping me up.

Everything in me was on fire.

My thoughts were like jolts of lightnin'. Rocketin' through my head. I couldn't think straight. Everything was jumbled up. Confused. And all I could see were heat waves coming from the floor, the walls, everywhere.

Once I was on my feet, I didn't care what I'd said or what I'd promised. I wasn't gon' take my clothes off.

Period.

I just wasn't.

And I wasn't gon' let this trick keep disrespectin' me like I wasn't nothin'.

Like the only thing that mattered was what she wanted; and what I wanted didn't mean a thing.

Like I ain't have the right to say no.

I wasn't garbage.

And I was done wit' e'rybody tossin' me around like stray dog shit. "Hell no, I ain't takin' nothin' off!" And right after I said that, I gathered every ounce of spit I could, from the pit of my gut, hocked Officer Washington dead in her beet-red face, and watched it drip over her shocked eyes, thin lips, and slide down her veiny neck.

6

The Bridge is Over

"Are you aware that the prosecutor wants to throw the entire book at you? Lock you up until you're 21? You realize that's six years? Two years for assault with a deadly weapon and four years for not keeping your spit where it belongs, in your mouth."

That was my public defender's introduction. She ain't state her name. Didn't ask me mine. Didn't shake my hand. Didn't ask me why I was lumped up like this. She just waltzed into the empty courtroom, with Nana behind her, like hot shit on a Gucci stick, announcin' that I was goin' to hell in a handbasket.

Nana looked me over as I sat at the defense table with the sheriff officer standin' next to me.

Nana frowned and said, "Dear God, somebody has finally kicked yo' li'l behind." She shook her head, causing the sanctified lace doily she had pinned to the top of her wig to shift to the left. Then she folded her navy pleated skirt beneath her and flopped down on the bench directly behind me. She leaned forward and said over my shoulder, "You can't help yourself, can you? Everywhere you go you gotta let the monkey-dog out! No matter what I tried to teach you, you just gon' do the opposite. Now you in jail showin' off. But you gon' learn. 'Cause them dykes and them guards gon' turn you out."

I huffed. Sat up straight in my chair, turned around, and looked her dead in the face. "That's what you came here for? To talk about the dykes and the guards?"

Nana pointed into my face. "I'm here because they keep calling me. Plus, I need some help wit' that snotty nose li'l baby you just up and left at my house. Now hush up being disrespectful. This lady is here tryna help you, and you just showin' your bare ass."

The thought of my baby pushed a hard lump into my throat. I looked at my attorney and said, "I need to see my baby! I need to get outta here!"

She never looked at me; instead she popped open her brown leather briefcase and said, "Well, perhaps you should've considered that before you spit in Officer Washington's face and made your case ten times harder for me to fight." She closed her briefcase, then leafed through a file.

"Excuse you? Harder for you to fight?" She still wasn't lookin' at me, so I hammered on the table. She snapped her neck around, and I continued. "You got this twisted. Ain't nobody fightin' for me but me. I'm the one who couldn't walk the street without e'rybody eyein' me like I was crazy because Munch lied and said I was a rat!"

"And so what?" my attorney said, clearly not giving a damn. "People call each other names all the time. Call her a name back or, better, be the bigger person and walk away."

"Amen!" Nana said.

My attorney continued. "You don't drag someone off of a city bus, slice their face, and try to kill them."

"Hello, somebody!" Nana waved her hands to the heavens.

"You can stop right there. Is you askin' me if I dragged her off the bus and sliced her face? Or is you just sidin' wit' the cops?"

My attorney batted her false lashes and frowned. "Don't be ridiculous. I represent you. What side do you think I'm on?"

I mimicked her couldn't-care-less shoulder shrug. "I don' know. 'Cause you came up in here yellin' about how I treated the CO, like she sent you on a mission to check me. How about you ask *me* how they treatin' *me* in jail? So I can tell you how, for the last two days, they had me tied down in a restraint chair, in a paper gown, with a spit guard over my mouth! Didn't even allow me to make a phone call, and e'rybody knows you get at least one of those! They just been pushin' me around. Treatin' me like I'm on Death Row!"

"You're not on Death Row. However, you are in jail."

"I know that, but dang! And I thought you were *my* attorney. You actin' like you should be sittin' at the prosecutor's table. You ain't asked me my name, told me yours, or asked me how I got these bruises on my arms." I held my arms out. "Or why I got these hickeys on the side of my face." I turned to the left. Then to the right. "Or why I got a lump on the back of my head. You ain't asked me nothin'. You just came at me crazy, tellin' me how I'ma be in jail forever."

My attorney sighed, looked at me, and held her right hand out. "Let's start again. My name is Sheryl Blakely." We shook hands, and she continued. "I'm a public defender. I've been assigned to represent you. And I never said you were going to jail forever."

"My name is Yvette Simmons. And you said six years. May as well be forever. Especially for somethin' I didn't even do."

Sheryl smirked. "Well, one thing you did do was spit in Officer Washington's face, and that's a charge."

I sucked my teeth. "That trick deserved the ounce of spit she got."

"And what you deserve is a few years in jail. But I'm trying to get the court to give you a chance here."

I couldn't believe she said that. "A chance? Really? I can't tell. Feels like you already got me tried and convicted. You ain't said nothin' about me gettin' outta here today and gettin' back to my baby."

"It doesn't work like that." She lowered her voice, as the prosecutor walked in, nodded at us, then sat down at her table.

"Well, how does it work?" I whispered back.

"You can plead innocent..."

"Which I am."

"Then you can take this to trial. Or..."

"Or what?"

"Plead guilty and let me speak with the prosecutor about a deal."

"Would I have to go to jail?"

"You may."

"And lose my baby! Hell no! I ain't break no laws!" I looked at the prosecutor and rolled my eyes. "Somebody call you a rat and tell people you a snitch, you handle 'em. E'rybody know that! And if some ho disrespect you, I don't care where it's at or where they from, then you deal with 'em. E'rybody know that too! Friend or no friend. CO or no CO."

"You need to lower your voice," Sheryl said sternly.

"All rise," the sheriff's officer said as the judge walked in and took his seat. "Judge Randall presiding."

"So, you really want this to go to trial?" Sheryl asked in a hush tone, as we stood up.

"Yes, I do."

She shook her head. "Fine."

"Counsels, state your credentials for the record," Judge Randall said.

"I'm Prosecutor Mildred Jones. Representing the state."

"I'm Sheryl Blakely. Public defender. Representing Yvette Simmons."

Judge Randall looked to his left. "Bailiff, please swear in the defendant."

"Raise your right hand," the bailiff said. "Do you swear or affirm to tell the truth, the whole truth, and nothing but the truth?"

"Yeah."

"State your name for the record."

"Yvette Simmons."

"You may be seated."

The judge looked at Sheryl and said, "Counsel Blakely, how does your client wish to plead?"

"Not guilty." She huffed, like she'd been defeated. She looked over to Nana, then back to the judge. "Your Honor, this is my client's grandmother, and she wishes to address the court."

Nana stood up and the bailiff swore her in. I could tell by the look on her face she was about to say somethin' stupid. "Good morning, Ya Honor. I'm Evangelist Darleen Carter. I bring you and the courtroom greetings from the Holiness Tabernacle Followers of Christ. I'm sure I look familiar to you." She paused and when the judge didn't say nothin', she carried on. "I was just in your courtroom a few months ago with my granddaughter, Isis. Now I'm in here with a new derelict, Yvette. First, let me make this clear: Yvette is not my granddaughter. I would say she's a family friend, who I let call me *Nana*, as a courtesy. My son brought her stray of a mother home, and one day I looked up and he'd left me with her litter."

"Ma'am," the judge said, like he'd already had enough of her, "please state why you're here."

Nana looked taken aback. "I'm here because this public defender keeps calling me." She pointed to Sheryl. "She's been calling me nonstop saying Yvette needs a guardian, in case the court releases her today."

"So you're here to take her home?" the judge asked.

"Oh, no. No, sir. Yvette's been causing me hell since the first time she said hello. She cannot dot my door again. I'm cleaning house. And the last thing I need is Yvette as a guest. She's lived wit' me, on and off, for five, long, drawn-out, and miserable years.

"Yvette needs help. She's a thief. She lies. She's trampy. She's violent. And the public defender told me that just the other day Yvette spat in one of the prison guard's faces! No, I'm done here. What's next? She gon' spit in my face, and then I'm standing before you, charged with murder? I'm too old for that and prison ain't for me. So, I'm here today to make sure we're all on the same page." Nana looked around the courtroom. "Now, I've already made arrangements for Child Protective Services to come and get this baby Yvette left at my house, 'cause I will not be raising her. And this courtroom was my last stop. So hear me, and hear me well, this evangelist here has officially washed her hands of and has given this sixteen-year-old Jezebel, named Yvette, to the Lord."

"Where are her parents?" the judge asked.

"Somewhere needin' prayer. I'm sure her mother's in somebody's crack den or the back seat of some trick's Chevy. And I'm sure her daddy's a john or probably one of the mama's sick uncles. Hell, maybe even her brother."

"Do you know any of Yvette's family members?"

"I barely know Yvette, let alone her relatives. And I don't wanna know 'em. But one thing I do know is who ain't related to Yvette. And that's me and my family."

"That's enough, ma'am. You may be excused," the judge said, pointing to the court's double doors.

"Goodbye." Nana shoved the shoulder strap of her black leather purse up her arm, held her head up, and high stepped out the courtroom, the double doors swinging behind her. She never looked back. Never even glanced over her shoulder. Just walked out like the last thing she wanted me to see was her leavin' me behind.

The judge banged his gavel, grabbing my attention. "Yvette Simmons, you will be remanded until the next hearing."

What did he say?

The courtroom buzzed. The prosecutor stood up, shuffled through her files. She looked at the bailiff and told him to call the next case.

I wanted to ask somebody to repeat what the judge had just said, but they was all movin' about like I no longer existed, like we was no longer in the same moment.

My heart thumped, hard and fast, but the beat was fading.

Tears pounded against the backs of my eyes and burned their way down my cheeks.

One of the sheriff's officers ordered me to stand up so they could cuff and shackle me.

I didn't move.

That's when it hit me. The judge had said, "Remanded until the next hearing."

My vision blurred.

My heart died.

My stomach twisted into knots.

The knots dropped into my feet.

My whole body felt heavy.

I couldn't breathe.

I couldn't think.

All I could do was scream.

E'rybody was lookin' at me like I was crazy.

I wasn't crazy.

I wasn't.

I just needed somebody to understand that I had to get back to my baby! Otherwise I was gon' die.

And although I was born in hell, I wasn't ready to be burned to death.

Then Kamari wouldn't have nobody!

The last thing I wanted was for my baby girl to be like me.

I kept telling myself to shut up, 'cause the screams made me look like I was buggin'.

I wasn't buggin'.

I just couldn't stop screamin'.

E'rybody in the courtroom, even the judge, seemed frozen by my shrieks. Like nobody knew if I was gon' throw a chair or drop dead.

Shut up! Stop screaming! Relax! Think! Stop screaming!
But the screams wouldn't stop.

"I can't stay in here!" I finally spat out. "I gotta get back to my baby! You can't keep me here! You can't!"

The judge didn't say a word. He just stared. Two sheriff officers yanked my arms behind me, while I did my all to twist outta their hold. "You don't get it! I can't be away from my baby! Please don't do this! She's all I got! I don't have nobody else! She don't have nobody else! Please let me go! Please! I need to leave! Please!"

My cries echoed off the walls, throughout the court-room, and down the hall, as the two officers whisked me back to the bullpen and left me in the middle of the cold concrete floor to die.

7

Holy Intellect

"What's my name? Tell e'rybody who I am? Is you serious?" I said in disbelief.

"Yes, I am," Ms. Conyers, the tall, lanky, brunette social worker said to me, as she stood in the middle of the room, smilin' and lookin' stupid.

I'd been locked up for two solid weeks and in order to keep my sanity, I kept to myself and focused on mindin' my bissness. But today, of all days, when I felt like if somebody looked at me wrong, it was gon' be on, one of the COs ordered me to group therapy, swearin' it was mandatory.

So I sat in a circle, in a sunshine-painted concrete room, with two barred windows and four simple broads. Two of 'em who twirled each other's hair, one who thought she was a boy, and another one who was clearly dope sick.

All of 'em pretty much did they own thing until I said, "My first name is Accused of Assault With a Deadly Weapon. And my last name is For Supposedly Beatin' Somebody's

Ass." Then they all sat up at attention and all eyes was suddenly on me.

The boy-girl giggled, looked over at the twirlin' twins, and said, "Told y'all that was her." She looked back over to me. "You the one who dragged Munch at the bus stop? I heard about you. Heard you housed her, yo. But I also heard you was a rat and that I needed to watch you."

Dope-sick jumped in. "That e'rybody needed to watch you."

If we was on the street, I'da already smacked both of these hoes, but since we wasn't and I wasn't in the mood to be thrown in the hole, I swallowed the urge to palm-kick the man-chick and the fiend. Instead, I looked at the boy-girl and said, "S'pose I said I heard you was a rat, too." Then I looked over at the fiend. "And s'pose I said I heard you was in the alleyway on yo' knees e'ryday? Then what? That make it true?"

"I ain't no rat, yo," the boy-girl said.

The fiend didn't say nothin'.

I continued. "How I know that?"

"'Cause I said it. And I wouldn't never do that!" The boy-girl huffed, heated.

I shrugged. "So? And? People say a lot of things. E'rybody say they ain't a rat, but somebody rattin', and usually the main ones who say they wouldn't never do that, be the main ones doin' it."

"Don't call me no rat, yo." She stood up and Ms. Conyers stepped in front of her.

"That's enough, Myesha," Ms. Conyers said. "Now sit down." She paused. And the boy-girl sucked her teeth, then flopped back down in her seat. "It's one thing to disagree; after all, working out disagreements is healthy. But

you cannot get into each other's faces. I have zero toler-
ance for that. Now..." She looked over to me. "Perhaps
we should start again. Please tell the group your name and
a little about yourself."

I pressed my elbows into my thighs and leaned forward.
"What you wanna know about me for? Don't none of y'all
up in here care. Far as y'all concerned, my name is Assault.
Ain't that's how y'all see me? As a charge?" I leaned back in
my chair and flicked her off.

"No," Ms. Conyers said. "I see you as a scared young
lady who expresses her hurt by way of anger."

I rolled my eyes. "Y'all kill me, always tryna evaluate
and diagnose somebody. Don't nobody wanna hear all
that. And I'm not angry."

"Then what would you call it?"

"Pissed off."

"Why are you pissed off?"

I smirked. *She was workin' e'ry one of my nerves.* "Why
you think I'm pissed off? You ain't crazy. You ain't stupid.
I'm pissed off 'cause I'm in here. 'Cause y'all got me
locked up like I did something wrong. Tryna blame e'rything on me."

"Trying to blame what on you?"

"Look, I ain't gon' recap that. You know how y'all do."

"Who's *y'all*."

"You, the police, the prosecutor, my PD; at the end of
the day, all y'all the same. Lockin' folks up for a paycheck."

"That is true," the fiend agreed. "That's how I feel too."

"Me, too," one of the twirlin' twins said. "Nobody really
hear you. Nobody really listen to you. 'Cause if they did,
they would see that this ain't the place to be."

Ms. Conyers nodded, like she was interested in what

we'd just said. "Okay, well let me ask you all this: What part did you all play in getting here? Surely you did something to bring you to this moment."

I sat up in my seat and pointed. "See, told you. Now it's our fault that we locked up?" I eyed the group. "Now we the reason we in here. So I'm in here 'cause of my actions, is what you sayin'? Not 'cause some bird was out in the streets runnin' her mouth, ruinin' my rep, and I couldn't even walk down my own block without watchin' my back and lookin' over my shoulder. Not 'cause somebody put my life in jeopardy for somethin' I didn't even do. Nah, she's the victim. But me, I'm public enemy number one."

"No one said that," Ms. Conyers replied.

"You ain't gotta say it, to say it. Listen, so what if I dragged somebody for lyin' on me? What's the problem wit' that? That's how it goes. You come for me, I shoot you. Period. E'rybody knows that." I looked around the group and they was all noddin' they heads in agreement. I continued. "Yet, y'all got me sittin' up in here wit' a buncha chicks I don't even know, wantin' me to spill my guts, like that's normal. Hell, no! You don't care that my name is Yvette. That I'm sixteen. A child without a mother and a mother without a child. That I don't have nobody. Y'all don't care about that. All y'all see me as some blade-swingin' maniac wit' anger problems, who needs to be locked up. Well, that ain't who I am."

"Who are you?" Ms. Conyers asked.

"First name Accused of Assault with a Deadly Weapon and last name For Supposedly Beatin' Somebody's Ass."

8

Microphone Checker

A month later

L ately, I'd been tryin' not to sleep.
But I kept failin'.

And fallin' victim to stupid dreams. That made me think
I was back wit' my baby, holdin' her, kissin' on her, blow-
in' bubbles into the folds of her chubby brown belly and
makin' her cough up wet giggles.

Then *bang!*

I'd wake up to the sound of the COs unlockin' the cell
doors and orderin' e'rybody to mess-hall for breakfast.

Which I half ate.

Mainly 'cause the eggs was orange and runny.

The oatmeal was tree-bark brown and stiff.

The bacon was pork and I didn't eat swine.

The bread was the only thing I wasn't afraid to swallow,
and most of the time, that was stale.

But I had to eat somethin'.

After breakfast, it was against the rules to go back to your cell. If you wasn't in school, then you had to sit in the rec room and watch these numbered skeezers pretend the only thing that mattered was hip-hop, break dancin', LL Cool J, UNO, which one of they dudes was worth doin' time for, and the community dick they left chillin' on the block.

Ignorant broads.

Wit' no dreams.

No responsibilities.

No thoughts.

Just silly.

Sittin' in here talkin' and laughin' wit' the COs, like this was Showtime at the Apollo and not jail.

Me. I still ain't talk to none of these lunatics, 'cause I wasn't in here to make no friends. I was just here.

Unwanted tears filled my eyes.

But I couldn't cry. I ain't need none of these chicks thinkin' I was soft, then try and test me, and I'd have to turn into a tick-tick-bomb and pop off.

"Simmons!" Officer Wallace, one of the COs, yelled my name from across the room. Of course, the happy jailbirds took pause so they could look and see what I was doin'. The twirlin' twins rolled they eyes, 'cause they couldn't stand me. So I gave 'em a look that dared 'em to leap. When they didn't move, I walked past 'em and said, under my breath, "I ain't think so."

"What?" I stood in front of Officer Wallace, who *always* sat in a rollin' chair, 'cause she was too lazy to walk.

"Don't what me, Simmons," she said firmly, like she was lookin' for a reason to get up. "I ain't Washington."

I know you ain't Washington, 'cause if you was, I'da

kicked you outta that chair by now. "Yes, Officer Wallace."

She clicked her tongue. "That's what I thought. Your PD is here." She looked over at one of the other COs. "Johnson, escort Simmons to room two."

The moment I laid eyes on Sheryl, in her black-power pants suit, hair feathered and curled to perfection, and her brown leather briefcase sitting next to her sunglasses, my attitude inched toward the ceilin'. I hadn't seen her since the guards carted me outta the courtroom a month and a half ago. And now she wanted to show up, grinnin', askin' me how I was doin', and holdin' her hand out.

"You seriously trippin'." I sat down in one of the chairs and reared back, leavin' her hand hangin'. Then I looked toward the window and for a moment wished I could break the glass and squeeze through the bars.

She sat down in the chair across from me. "Look, I know you may think I've forgotten about you..."

"Yep. Pretty much."

"Well, I haven't."

"Umm-hmm."

"Could you turn around and look at me?" she asked.

Oh, now she wanted me to look her way. I pursed my lips, rolled my eyes, and gave her a quick glance. "What?" Then I looked back out the window.

She sighed. "Listen, Yvette. Today is not the day that I've elected to put up with your hood-rat attitude."

Hood rat?

She carried on. "I have a million things to do, and a million and one other cases I need to attend to."

"Then what is you here for? Lookin' for gratitude? You

came to see me. I ain't call you. So today *ain't the day* that *I've elected* to put up with *your* fake-ass esquire attitude."

She took a deep breath. Held it. Then pushed it out and said, "You know, you have a right to be angry. However, you do not have a right to be angry with me."

I turned around in my chair and stared at her. Clearly, she's was tryna social-work me.

She continued. "I haven't done anything to you."

"You ain't done nothin' for me either. I asked you to get me outta here, yet I'm still sittin' here, rockin' this orange jumpsuit like it's the bomb. My baby's in foster care! CPS writin' me letters and askin' me have I ever considered adoption! And now you up in here tryna tell me I have a right to be angry, but not with you? Trick, please. Who is you, but some public pretender, collecting a paycheck from the same state that's trying to take my baby and send me to jail for six years!"

"You may not believe it, but I care."

"Yeah, yeah. My mother cared. Nana cared. Isis cared. Munch cared. Cali cared. E'rybody cared, but e'rybody gave me they behind to kiss."

"Listen, I met with the prosecutor."

"What, y'all had lunch or somethin'? 'Cause I know y'all homegirls." I twisted my lips.

Sheryl frowned. "We're not *homegirls*; we're colleagues. And we met to discuss your case. After everything that happened in court, she felt for you and offered you a deal."

I shrugged. "And?"

Sheryl hesitated. "Well, you'd have to plead guilty."

I should slap this heifer. "What kind of deal—if you don't get outta my face wit' that. What I look, stupid to you? I ain't doin' that."

"Hear me out. The prosecution can't prove who cut the girl, and CO Washington is willing to drop the charges."

"And that means what?"

"That means that since the fight is the only thing they can prove, because you confessed to it, you'll only be charged with disorderly conduct. But there's a catch."

"What is it?"

"You have to spend a year in what's called a professional parent home."

"A group home?!"

"It's not a group home, per se. It's a professional parent home, so you're not in a facility. You're actually living in someone's house. There's no staff. Just someone who's considered a parent."

"So since the state can't find my mama, they just gon' assign me one. Psst, please."

"Pretty much, and if you do not do well there, then you will either be back here, in jail, without your daughter, or in a group home facility, also without Kamari. One last thing, the professional parent home is in Norfolk, Virginia. The prosecutor's giving you a week to decide. It's the only one CPS could find that would take you and..."

"I don't need a week to decide, 'cause I ain't goin' to no professional parent, group home, or whatever it is. I'm not leavin' my baby for a year! And what the heck is a Norfolk? Is that even on this planet? I ain't goin' there. And, furthermore, if I'm only being charged with disorderly conduct, then I should be able to take my baby and walk."

"Not exactly. You're still a minor. The state of New Jersey is responsible for you. And CPS is not going to just *give you* your daughter, then stand back and watch two minors walk off into the sunset."

"First of all, I'm grown. And I never said I was gon' walk off into the sunset. But if that's what I wanted to do, Kamari is *my* child, not CPS's, not the state's—so they should all just mind they bissness, while I take my baby and handle mines. Like I been doin'."

"It doesn't work that way. CPS and the state…"

"Psst, please. CPS? The state? They ain't never cared about where I lived before. Now they got an opinion? Where was they when my mother had us squattin'? When we was sleepin' in cars, corners, closets, alleyways, livin' with this one, livin' with that one, when I woke up one day and Nana was lookin' in my face? Where was CPS and the state then? Now, all of a sudden, I gotta listen to them, when they ain't never gave a damn until now? Girl, boo. I'ma do me. And what you can do, is tell 'em I said gimme me my baby and step off."

Sheryl huffed. "Okay. Is that what you want?"

"That's what I said."

"Then fine. I'll do just that. I'll tell them you said step off. But then what? What will you do after that? Take this to trial? And lose? Because you will not win. Officer Washington will happily testify against you. And maybe the prosecution can't prove who cut Munch today. But by the time they get her up on that stand, she cries, and tells the court the horrors of being attacked on her way to school, you will be found guilty. And you will serve every bit of time the court gives you.

"Then what happens to Kamari? In six years, she will not be a baby. She will be school age, probably adopted, calling someone else 'Mommy,' with little-to-no memory of you."

I shot her a warning eye. "You going too far! And if I'm found guilty it's 'cause you triflin' and didn't try."

"So, let's assume you're found innocent. The state lets you take Kamari and walk. Then what?"

I smirked. "Whatchu mean, then what? I'ma take care of my baby."

"How?"

"I'ma get a job."

"Really? Where? When's the last time you were in school?"

Last year. Ninth grade. I stopped goin' 'cause the only thing poppin' was the hallway and I wasn't beat. Plus, I had a baby that Nana wouldn't keep. I looked at Sheryl and frowned. I wasn't about to give her the satisfaction of even answerin' that question.

She continued. "Obviously school is a distant memory. So that leads me to the next question: Do you have any skills?"

Silence.

Sheryl carried on. "Whether you know it or not, no answer is an answer. And your silence leads me to believe that your skill set, at this moment, consists of stealing penny candy from the bodega and boosting clothes from the mall."

"Don't try and play me out."

"I'm trying to help you out. Now tell me, can you type? Are you familiar with computers? Because they're taking over. Do you work well with people? Can you get along with them or is dragging folks off the bus and slicing their faces your expertise?"

"You buggin' and I ain't gotta listen to this!" I stood up and so did Sheryl.

"Sit your behind back down!" she said.

I didn't know if it was the base in her voice, or the shock of her comin' at me in a frustrated fit, that forced me to listen. But I did.

I sucked my teeth and fell back down in my seat.

She continued. "I have had enough of you! You think you're the only one who had it hard? You think you're the only one who didn't have the best mother, the best father, or the best circumstances? Well you're not. 'Cause guess what? I got a caseload of disappointed, pissed off, and broken-hearted juveniles. And, no, life isn't fair. But we all get the same twenty-four hours, and you can either do the right thing or you can fight for street cred and end up in jail, or dead."

She gathered her briefcase. "Choice is yours. However, if I were you, I'd accept the plea deal, get out of that distasteful orange jumpsuit, get my butt on that bus, go to Norfolk, Virginia, to that professional parent home—because it's the only one that agreed to let you bring Kamari. Then when I got there, I'd act like I had some goddamn sense and make the best out of it!"

Sheryl slid on her sunglasses and turned toward the door. "But what do I know? After all, you're grown and I'm only a public pretender."

9

Bust a Move...

*A **week** later...*

This. Was. Some. Bull.

Not only did CPS and the state of New Jersey force me and Kamari into what felt like some witness protection program, they had us gallopin' down I-95 in some musty behind, hot Trailways bus, where the bathroom tissue was soggy and the gray tiled diamonds on the bathroom floor glistened from old and new piss.

And that was the best part of the trip. Here's where hell stepped in: For nine hours, we was crammed up with a thousand other people. And by the time we stopped in Delaware, Maryland, D.C., and fifty-eleven places in Virginia, e'rything and e'rybody smelled like mornin' breath and midnight ass, includin' this red-haired, Valley girl social worker sent to escort me, who didn't know the meaning of *shut up*.

Thennnnnn, just when I thought I'd left the hood in Newark, we arrived at the Norfolk bus station and was greeted by hustlers, pimps, tricks, and hoes.

It was ten p.m., and Janette, my social worker, was obviously scared to death 'cause she had us holdin' hands and sprintin' over to the Hertz car rental booth, like a triplet of OJs. Afterwards, we checked out a hot pink Aries K, and Janette had us creepin' down Church Street like two misplaced junkies and a baby lookin' to cop.

Noooowwwww, we was on a tree-lined street, and there was no apartment buildings. No two, three, or four-family houses, only one-family dwellings. And none of them was boarded up, burned up, or abandoned. They was all different sizes, some with one story and others with two.

We stood on the steps of a two-story white house, with hunter green shutters, an air conditioner hangin' out the living room window drippin' water, and two light brown, corduroy recliners on the front porch. And some old lady, about forty-five or fifty, who was a little taller than me, maybe about five-three, with skin the color of the evening sun, amber freckles sprinkled across her nose. and high cheeks, a head full of pink sponge rollers, wide hips, and a huge bosom, smilin' at me, as she said in full Virginian twang, "Welcome home. You can call me Aunt Glo."

Then she boldly lifted Kamari, who'd been standin' next to me, onto her hip, squeezed my baby and tickled the side of her neck. "You just as cute as you wanna be. I'ma call you Butter, 'cause you're my little butterball." She tickled her again and Kamari laughed, like she was having the time of her two-year-old life.

All I could think was, *Oh. Hell. No.*

I'd seen this smile before.

I'd heard this same ole greetin'—*Welcome home! You can call me Aunty, Mama, Nana*...

New people.

Same old bullshit.

And my same old mercy tossed at somebody else's wide feet. And, yeah, she seemed like she was nice enough, and yeah, Kamari went to her without hesitation. But Kamari was a baby. I was grown, so I knew better. Plus, I'd been the new kid in a new hood one too many times before. And just 'cause this was a new state and a new city, ain't mean I was suddenly beat for this street. 'Cause at the end of the day—whether the housemother was tall, short, fat, skinny, light, dark, or in-between—the look in they eyes was all the same and all said the same thing: *Don't get too comfortable, 'cause one of these days, when you least expect it, I'ma put you out.*

Therefore, her niceness ain't impress me. Actually, it pissed me off, and I wished she would just skip the honeymoon smile and get to the real deal.

I took Kamari out of her arms and tucked my baby onto my hip. Then I twisted my lips, twirled my index finger in the air, and set the record straight. "First of all, her name is Kamari, not Butter. Second of all, you not my aunt. We ain't gon' even start that. You'll never have me in court, disowning me and tellin' the judge I'ma family friend. I'm done with that. Now, outta respect, what I will call you is Ms. Glo."

I paused, and when she didn't say or do anything more than look at me like I was completely crazy, I carried on, "And third of all, this *ain't* my home. Me and my baby was sentenced to do a year here, and then we in the wind like

Flynn. Adios, Amiga. Hotep. Peace to the Middle East." I tossed up two fingers. "You feel me?"

Obviously, she didn't, 'cause all she did was look at Janette and say, "You wanna come in, 'cause I have a feeling you've had a long trip."

We walked into the living room, which was decorated with a soft brown leather living room set, plush beige carpet, a floor model TV, stereo system with extra large speakers in two corners of the room, and framed posters of Malcolm X, Marcus Garvey, and Martin Luther King hanging on beige, popcorn walls.

Janette looked at me and her eyes pleaded for me to play nice. All I could do was flip my hair over my shoulders and shake my head. Bump, Janette. She didn't have to live here. I did.

Kamari spotted Ms. Glo's small black dog and twisted to get out of my arms.

"It's okay; you can put her down," Ms. Glo said, all up in my bissness. "Princess plays well with children."

I sucked my teeth. "No, she don't need to be running around and then I gotta hear about her touchin' your stuff."

"It's just stuff. She's a baby; let her move around," Ms. Glo insisted.

"I *said no.*"

"So you gon' hold her forever?"

"No, just while I'm here."

"So you gon' hold her for a year?"

Breathe in.

Breathe out.

Just chill.

Maybe she don't mean no harm. You don't know her and she don't know you. "Like I said. No."

Janette gave Ms. Glo a nervous smile, then said, "On the ride here, I told Yvette all about your home and your wonderful reputation. The state of New Jersey and Child Protective Services appreciates you accepting Yvette into your fold. We have high hopes that this will be just what she needs to turn her life around and not get into any more trouble, drag anybody else off the bus, or get arrested again."

My eyes bucked. Did this heifer really just play me like that? I turned toward Janette and said, "For real? Seriously? So you just gon' tell all my bissness, like I'm not even standing here? Word. That's what we doin' now? Lettin' it all hang out. Well, okay then, let me just say this." I turned my attention to Ms. Glo. "Obviously, you heard a whole lot about me. And most of it is probably true. But that don't mean I'm all bad and that I'ma spend e'ry wakin' moment comin' for you."

"Well, thank God for small favors. I appreciate that," Ms. Glo said, tappin' her pink slipper–covered foot and foldin' her arms across her breasts, like she was interested in what else I had to say.

So I continued. "All I want to do is my time here, in peace."

"Sounds good to me. Do you wanna sing 'Kumbaya' and recite Bible verses in the mornings too?"

I paused. *Was she tryna make me cuss her out?* I tapped my foot. *Maybe I need to tell her that I fight old ladies too.*

I bit the inside of my cheek.

Just let it go.

But she got one mo' time...

I continued. "All I'm sayin' is that I don't want no static and no drama."

"A young woman with a plan; I like that."

I carried on. "Cool. I'm glad you do. So then let me just say this: The only way this whole arrangement gon' work is if you understand that I'm grown. Kamari is my baby and what I say to her goes. If she do somthin' you don't like, come tell me and I'll handle it. I also don't need nobody in your family talkin' crazy to me or it's gon' be a problem. You got an issue wit' me, then you tell me. I don't need yo' daughter, if you got one, steppin' to me. Another thing, respect my privacy and I'll respect yours. Don't ask me about myself or my family."

"And why is that?"

"'Cause this ain't personal. This is business."

10

Check Yo'self before You Wreck Yo'self...

I hated feelin' like this.
Straight up hated it.

Hated that e'ry mornin' I wondered if my mother was gon' walk through the door and say, "Come on, baby girl. Let's go."

The first time she took off I was about four, maybe five. She left me wit' a lady called Aunt Maxine, whom I couldn't stand. Not 'cause she wasn't nice. She just wasn't who I needed her to be. For six months, I couldn't breathe. Then one day, my mother showed up, I caught my breath, and we left.

After that, we was together for nine months. Then she sent me next door to stay with a neighbor. She came back a year later wit' a new man, a new baby, and a new smile.

We was good for two years. She had three more babies; we lost our apartment and squatted in an abandoned buildin'. Two months after that, the police put us out.

Then we lived in her car.

A homeless shelter.

A drug program that housed addicts and they kids.

A month later, we got kicked out and moved in with Nana.

Ma stuck around for two weeks; then she and her boyfriend went to cop and never came back.

That was six years ago. I was ten.

I'm sixteen now. I'm grown. I got sense enough to know that my mother ain't never gon' be more than wandering shit. I also know that her kids will never be enough to save her. It's not like she had us out of love. We was just five tragedies that happened to a fiend.

Yet, here I was in a whole other place, a whole other state, but always on edge, wonderin' if she was gon' walk through the door again.

Thennnnn, as if feelin' like that wasn't bad enough, I also found myself missin' Da Bricks.

I missed the heat of the early mornin' sun. The beat of an unannounced boombox suddenly blastin' through the courtyard, while somebody screamed, "Aye, yo, yo, what's good, homie!" While somebody else lifted up they window and answered, "Dammit, it's too early for that!"

I missed my old crew and the way we used to hang out, chill, and be ill. Spittin' stupid rhymes, break dancin', sittin' on the park bench, laughin', dreamin', plottin' and schemin'.

I cracked up at the thought of me and Isis stealin' Nana's rent money and Nana blamin' it on Stick. Then the time we got caught boostin' clothes from the mall.

Then me and Munch...

Munch...

I wish...

I sucked my teeth. Forget that. I didn't wish nothin'.

I flung away the tears that escaped from my eyes, and in an attempt to feel better, I turned over to snuggle with a sleepin' Kamari.

There was only one problem.

Wasn't no Kamari.

My heart dropped.

Don't panic.

She gotta be around here somewhere.

I sat up straight in bed and tossed my feet around to the floor; that's when I noticed that the bedroom door was open.

Ugh.

I slid on blue joggin' pants underneath my gown, slipped on a pair of socks, took two steps out of the room and there she was, in the kitchen. Wrapped in the arms of some high yellow, big booty, smilin' skank. And this skeezer had my baby suckin' on a piece of slimy pork bacon, with grease smeared across her warm brown cheeks. Kamari's hair was in two wild and curly ponytails, and her button-brown eyes were bright with surprise when she spotted me.

Kamari grinned, her mouth full of tiny bacon bits. "Hi, Mommy!" she said.

Before I could say anything, the skank said, "She is *soooooo* cute. I hope you don't mind me picking her up."

"Well, I do. But what I won't mind is you puttin' her down." I walked over and took my baby out of her arms. Then I reached for a napkin and wiped the bacon grease off of Kamari's face.

I drew in a breath to keep from smackin' this light-bright ho, and said, "Let me be clear: Me and my baby don't eat swine. So don't give it to her again. Next, I don't appreciate her bein' in here, and nobody asked me if she could leave the room. Especially since I don't leave my baby wit' random chicks."

"She's not a random chick. Her name's Tasha," Ms. Glo said, switchin' her wide behind past me and into the kitchen. She walked over to the stove, turned the burner on, and placed an iron skillet on the fire. She looked over to Tasha. "Hand me the butter out of the refrigerator."

She turned her attention back to me. "Yvette, Tasha has lived here for the last two years. She was only being nice, especially since you neglected to mention that you had a sign-out sheet for the baby. That wasn't listed as one of your rules last night. And neither was no swine; therefore, you are three bacon strips too late."

Now I was livid. "Three?"

"One. Two. Three. And what's the problem with eating pork? Religion? Allergy?"

"No and no," I snapped. "Me and my baby just don't eat it."

"Ooooh, I see. *Umm-hmm.* Nonsense." Ms. Glo poured pancake mix, water, and sour cream into a large mixin' bowl and stirred it up. Then she turned around to the stove and dumped two hunks of butter into the pan, like she didn't wanna hear nothin' else I had to say.

I smirked. "Listen, lady, didn't I tell you last night that Kamari was *my* baby."

Ms. Glo turned around, holding the mixin' bowl loosely in her hand. "Li'l girl, I appreciate the reminder, but I know exactly who she is."

She turned back to the stove, then poured pancake batter into the hot buttered pan. She continued. "My son is thirty-two years old, so one thing I'm not walking around here doing is claiming babies. Now I will take care of 'em, love 'em, and spoil 'em. Then I send 'em on their way."

"I got this. I don't even need you to do that much," I said.

"This morning was not about what you needed me to do. It was about this baby walking in here while Tasha and I were having breakfast, and saying, 'Eat, eat.' What would you have me do? Let her starve?"

"You could've woke me up."

She flipped over the pancakes. "Well, forgive me for thinking that you were up late last night and may have wanted your sleep." She took the pancakes out of the pan and slid them onto a plate. "Especially since you have to be up early for school tomorrow."

Pause.

School? "What?"

"School. You know, the place where the two teenagers, you and Tasha, who live here, must go." She poured more batter into the pan.

Five.

Four.

Three.

Kamari twisted in my arms, tryin' to get down. I shoved her further up my hip. "Look, when I agreed to come here, school wasn't a part of the deal. Therefore, I ain't goin'. Point blank, period."

Ms. Glo arched a brow. "Oh, really?" She flipped over the pancakes.

"Yeah, really."

"And why is that?"

"'Cause I don't have time for school. What I'ma do is

get me a job, so when this year is up I can step." Kamari continued to twist wildly in my arms.

"And just where you gon' step to, the welfare line? Would you put that child down?!" She walked over to me, took Kamari outta my arms, and placed her on the floor. "You need to..."

"I don't need you tellin' me what to do!" My intention was to snatch Kamari back into my arms, but she'd already climbed into one of the kitchen chairs, sat down, looked at Tasha and said, "Eat, eat."

Tasha didn't move.

But Ms. Glo, took a plate, cut up a pancake, drizzled maple syrup on it, and placed it in front of Kamari, who started eatin' that stupid pancake, with her hands, like it was the best thing she'd ever had.

"I don't need you in my bissness!" I snapped at Ms. Glo.

She hesitated. Looked up at the ceiling then back at me, and said, "No, what you need is a foot up yo' behind, but since we're just getting acquainted, I'm not gon' be rude. But you're pushin' it."

"You better..."

"The only thing I better do is stay black, pay taxes, and die. That's it. Everything else is an option."

"Listen..."

"I don't have to listen to you, li'l girl. I'm fifty years old; you're only sixteen. What could you possibly have to tell me that I need to listen to? I run this. And it will be my way..."

"Or what, the highway? Is this the point where you put me out?"

"Put you out?" She frowned, sliding more pancakes onto a plate. "You're about to put yourself out 'cause obviously you don't wanna be here. Especially if you think you gon' run me. And another thing you obviously don't want is this baby. You must wanna give her away and have the state place her into another foster home."

What did she just say?

She locked eyes with me. "Yeah, I said it. You don't want her. 'Cause if you did, then you wouldn't be up in here actin' nutty as hell 'cause somebody fed your baby breakfast! Are you crazy?" She paused, like she expected me to really answer that.

I didn't.

She continued. "You're lucky I didn't check you comin' through the door last night."

"If you had somethin' to say, you shoulda said it."

She sighed; clearly I was wearin' her out. She sighed again. "You know what, Yvette. Why don't you help us both out of this situation? Do both of us a favor; take yourself into the other room and call your social worker." She nodded, like that was a great idea. "Yeah, you do that. Tell her to come and get you, that you don't like it here, and would rather go back to jail."

I couldn't believe she went there. I sucked my teeth. "Don't put words in my mouth."

"Yeah, the social worker is exactly who you need, because I will not tolerate this. You're running up in here and speaking to me like this is yo' crib. Oh hell no! You can pack your bags and leave. Believe me, there are a million other teens lookin' to take yo' spot, who will come here and appreciate what I have to offer!"

"I don't..."

"Have no manners!" Ms. Glo interjected. "Not one. Nobody here has done anything to you, but you're standing in my face actin' like a fool. Now if you're looking for a way out, then the phone is in the other room. Make this easy for all of us and make your phone call. Tell CPS you wanna break your plea and go back to jail. And maybe when you get out, in six years, Kamari will be waiting for you, and maybe she won't. But you will not run me 'cause I don't owe you shit, not even a second damn chance."

Silence.

She continued, "Now the choice is yours. You wanna leave, then go and pack your bags." Ms. Glo looked at me, like she was tryna read my eyes for a decision.

I didn't move.

She carried on. "But if you wanna stay, then you need to understand this. I run a quiet ship. All this ruckus, hollerin', and fussin' gon' stop today. Right now. 'Cause if you ever speak to me like this again, you will be right back on that hot and pissy Trailways bus you rode in here on."

She looked at me like she was darin' me to say somethin'.

I didn't.

She continued. "Next, school. There's no room for negotiation. Every day there's school, you gon' be there. Now I've already arranged for you to be tested on the first day; providing you pass, you will be placed in your correct grade."

"I can't leave Kamari."

"I'ma keep Kamari. So you can shoot that excuse. Next up is your curfew."

Curfew?

"Curfew," she said like she had read my mind. "Nine p.m. on week days. One a.m. on weekends. Break it if you want to, and the social worker will be waitin' for you. Got that?"

Silence.

"I asked you a question."

"Yeah, I got it," I answered reluctantly.

"Thought so. 'Cause what you not gon' do is run my pressure up. Life is too short for that." She turned back to the stove and poured more pancake batter into the hot pan. "Now that we've gotten that straight, you want one or two pancakes?"

11

Can't Stand Rain

"Hey, girl," Tasha said, pushing her face into the crack of my bedroom door. She dropped her eyes to the floor, where Kamari played with her toys. They smiled at each other; then Tasha looked back to me. She popped her lips. "I was thinking, since we didn't exactly meet and greet under the best circumstances—'cause you know, that li'l incident in the kitchen wasn't all that pretty—that maybe we should try again."

I didn't even respond to that.

She continued. "I'm Tasha Monique Wright. Well, on most days. 'Cause on Mondays, I'm Tash-boogie. That's what my Roni-love, M.C. Swavey, calls me. He's a chocolate-Rican-rapper, girl. Don't worry, he got some friends. Now on Tuesdays and Wednesdays, I'm just Tasha. On Thursdays, I'm Tash-LaRock 'cause sometimes I be spittin' stupid-fresh rhymes in the skating rink parking lot; that's where everybody hangs out after school.

"On Thursdays, I'm Sweet Cheeks, 'cause I got me a li'l Chinese boo."

"Chinese?"

"Free fried rice and egg rolls, girl. Plus, he's cute."

"I guess."

"But on the weekends, I'm T-Love. And T-Love is single. 'Cause ain't nobody got time to be all ball and chained up. No, ma'am." She pushed the door completely open, invited herself in, and flopped down, Indian style, on the edge of my bed. "So tell me a little about yourself. Not that I was listening, but I heard Aunty Glo say something about jail." Her downward slanted eyes lit up like Christmas tree lights. "Do tell."

Tasha was extra bubbly. A little more bubbly than I was in the mood for. Her smile was a mile wide, her full lips were glossy and her butterscotch-colored skin shone. Her hair was styled in an asymmetrical, stacked bob, with a long tail hanging down her back. And her big behind made her look twice my size. I wondered where she was from. She had a southern accent, but there was somethin' about the way she spoke that let me know she wasn't from the south.

I almost smiled at her. Instead, I bit my bottom lip, then sucked it in.

She placed her hand on my shoulder, givin' me a playful push. "Come on, girl, you gon' be mad forever?"

"Nope. Just while I'm here." I reached for the two pancakes I had on the nightstand and took a bite. I hated that the pancakes were good. At least if they were nasty, I could say I hated Ms. Glo and her nasty pancakes.

Tasha said, "Look, I get it. I was pissed off when I came here too."

"I can't tell."

"Well I was. This was the last place I wanted to be, but I didn't have a choice."

"What did you do? Why are you here?" Tasha paused and twisted her lips. The look in her eyes said she was wonderin' if she should tell me or not. So I said, "Don't nothin' surprise me. Trust. Not pimps, not hoes, not fiends, and definitely nothin' in-between. So spill it; what did you do?"

"I used to run away."

I curled the corner of my upper lip. "That's it? You in here for runnin' away? You couldn't learn to sit still?"

"It's more than that. I was in a gang too." She tossed up a sign.

"West *siiide*," I said jokingly, surprisin' myself that I had any laughter left. "Sexed in?"

"Hell no. I ain't no bimbo. Hand-to-hand combat."

Impressed, I gave her a nod and a crooked grin.

She continued. "I also held up a gas station."

"You get any money?"

"Not really. All the cat had on him was fifty dollars."

"Ski mask or no ski mask?"

"No ski-mask. And a .22."

"Damn. All that for fifty dollars?"

"I know, right? Pitiful. And I sold dope and weed."

"Word?"

"Word."

"You was slangin' or you was runnin'?" I asked.

"Slangin'. Had my own corner and everything."

"Oh word."

"And I stabbed my mother's boyfriend."

"Well, dang," I said, surprised. "Don't tell me you stabbed your mother too?"

"No, I ain't stab my mother."

"Just checkin'. So what else you do?" I asked, now feelin' like a saint.

"That's it."

"Don't you think that's enough? So why did you stab your mother's boyfriend?"

"Cuz that sucker stole my stash and then got high with it."

"Whaaaat? I know he in darkness."

"No. It didn't get that far. My mother walked in on me, called the police, and told them I was trying to kill her boyfriend. And, well, the rest is Aunty Glo history."

"So when do you go back home?"

"I don't know. Maybe never. I had to be here for a year. It's been two, and Aunty Glo has never asked me to leave and I don't want to go."

"What about your mother?" I asked.

"I love my mother, but when it comes to men, she's weak. Plus, we never got along. I talk to her sometimes, but life is better with us not living together."

"Well, after a year, me and my baby outta here."

"You going back home to your mother?"

I paused. "A mother? What's that?"

Tasha nodded, like she didn't know how to answer that, so she said, "Okay. Your turn. Now what did you do?"

"Not as much as you."

We laughed and she said, "*Umm-hmm*. I bet. What you do?"

"I dragged a girl off the bus and beat her down."

"Why?"

"She said I was a snitch."

"Well, I know what name I won't be callin' you." Tasha giggled. "So what else you do?"

"That's it."

"That's it?"

"Pretty much. Unless you count the times I used to boost."

"From where?"

"The mall."

"I know you got some fly gear." She chuckled. "You still do that?"

"Girl, bye. I ain't tryna go back to jail."

"I hear that...anyway enough of all that. Tell me this, where are you from? 'Cause your accent is a li'l different."

"Jersey. Brick City."

"Word?" she asked, excited. "I'm from Compton. California, baby."

"Okay. I didn't think you were from Norfolk."

"Nope, I'm not. But I hope to make Norfolk my home forever."

"*Hmph*, well, good luck with that."

"Check it, Yvette. I know we just met, and I know you ain't ask me for no advice, but just let me say this: Right now Aunty Glo is all we got."

"Negative. First, she's not my aunt. And second, maybe *Ms*. Glo is all you got, but when my time is up, I'm outta here."

"All I'm sayin' is, while you're here, make the best of it. Give her a chance. She ain't all bad."

Maybe Tasha had a point. But then again, maybe she didn't. "Look, I'ma just go with the flow."

"I feel you. You gotta do whatever works for you."

"Exactly."

"I do have another question to ask you," she said.

"What's that?"

"Do you like hip-hop? 'Cause Dough E. Fresh gon' be in town and we gon' need to be in the house, baby!"

12

Gas Face

The next morning

"Aye, yo, shawtie! C'mere!" dropped from the air the moment me and Tasha stepped onto Carver High's crowded school yard.

My crisp white, high-top Reeboks screeched in the middle of the concrete, as I sank my eyes into some dude I'd never seen before. He was posted a few steps away beneath the basketball net. "Who's that?" I asked Tasha, as the mysterious cutie stared back at me.

"That's Brooklyn's crazy butt. But don't worry about him, he's nuts."

I looked back over to Brooklyn and quietly pulled him in. Fresh fade, deep chocolate skin, shadow beard, eyes the color of desert sand. "Brooklyn? That's his real name?"

Tasha rubbed clear roll-on lip gloss across her lips, then popped 'em. "Yep. And his mama's named Queens."

"Lies. For real?"

She laughed. "No. His mama's name is Brenda. They live down the street from us."

"Okay..." I drifted into a Brooklyn trance, put under by his smile and soft wink.

Tasha tapped me on the shoulder. "Did you hear me?"

I blinked. "No. What did you say?"

"I *said* we could always walk over there and see what he wants."

"Chile, boo. What I look, beat to you?" I rolled my eyes at Brooklyn, flicked my wrist, and turned around, givin' him my back to look at. I said to Tasha, "Is that how y'all say good morning down here, 'Aye, yo, shawtie, c'mere?' and what the heck is a shawtie?"

"Being called *shawtie* is like a compliment. It's like bein' called *boo* or *baby-girl*. Or like y'all say up north, *Ma*. But don't pay him no mind."

"Why?"

"He ain't shit." She waved her hand. "He used to go with this girl named Alesha. And Alesha is friends with my girl Reesie. And Reesie told me that Brooklyn was a square, a dud, and a clown."

"Word?"

"Word. But. He is a cutie."

I tossed on a look of disgust. "He ain't all that; he looks all right. Plus, I don't have time for no country bama-square-dud-clowns. All I wanna do is pass this placement test and focus on stayin' here for the rest of the day, without sneakin' out the back door and bouncin'."

"Well you better put your game face on, 'cause he's walking this..."

"Yo, Tasha, you wanna introduce us to ya girl?" fell over my shoulder.

My heart stopped.

Brooklyn.

Ugh!

God.

Breathe.

Chill.

Just turn around, hold a straight face, look at him and say, Excuse you?

Brooklyn towered over my four eleven frame, and it took everything in me not to smile up at him; instead, I arched my back, unintentionally makin' my C-cups bounce. I looked him over from the braids going straight back in his hair, his Kelly-green Adidas sweat suit, to the white Stan Smith Adidas on his feet.

I peeped over at his two homies. One was short like me and held a boom box on his right shoulder, dressed in Cross Color blue jeans, a dark gray Member's Only jacket, and a red Bermuda Kango. Then I looked over at his friend, whose name shoulda been Whack-Skee, wit' his Gumby haircut, black-rimmed glasses, a red-and-black lumberjack shirt, and black overalls—one leg pushed up and the other down.

Three suckers.

I popped off. "Yo, for real, son," I said to Brooklyn. "You off the meat rack. Where I'm from, you get done walkin' up on me and my homegirl like that. You lucky I don't call my homies an 'em to come through and see about yo' bama behinds!"

Brooklyn chuckled in disbelief. "Oh, you a city girl, huh? So what you think? We slow down here or somethin'? Check it, you can bring your homies if you want too. But just know that when they go home, it's gon' be with their eyes closed."

"Whatever, and anyway, I know you saw me flip you off. Yet, you ova here in my face." My eyes scanned his homies. "And I know y'all slow, dumb, retarded asses saw me too."

"Hold on, baby-girl. Chill wit' all that," Brooklyn said. "It's all good over here, shawtie. My homie spotted you with Tasha and thought you were cute." He pointed to Whack-Skee. "And I did too, 'til you opened your rat trap."

I sucked my teeth and spat out a quick comeback. "Rat trap? Boy, please. And for your information, I'm nobody's baby girl..."

Brooklyn interrupted. "You know what; you're right. Forgive me, young man. I didn't mean to offend you, sir."

"*Ouuuuuuule!*" followed by a round of snickers came from the small crowd that had gathered around.

I knew I shoulda just let the argument go, but I couldn't. If I walked away now and didn't shut it down, sooner rather than later, e'rybody out here would be tryna test me, so I said, "Is that the best you got? What? You bleedin'? You need a tampon? Or your mama's tittie in your mouth? 'Cause you doin' a whole lot of cryin' right now."

"Daaaaaaang!" rang out from the same crowd.

The veins runnin' through Brooklyn's neck jumped and just when I thought he was gon' lose it, he smiled and said, "All this comin' from a trick. Did I walk past you on the corner or somethin'? What? You need a dollar? Here you go." He tossed a single at me.

Before I could even think of what I needed to do to level his dis, the school bell rang and mostly e'rybody, in-cluding Brooklyn and his boys, hustled inside.

Me and Tasha was the only ones left standing there. I did my best not to look as played as I felt.

After a few moments in tongue-tied silence, Tasha said, "*Umm*, listen, Yvette. All that was uncalled for."

"That's what I'm sayin'. Is he crazy, steppin' to me like that?"

"I'm not talking about Brooklyn. I'm talking about you. You did way too much. Down here, we keep it cute. You could've just told him your name or shot him a wave and we could've walked away. But you up here actin' like you're the Godmother with a ring for him to kiss." She shook her head.

"Is you crazy? You got this twisted. Who you need to check is ole boy."

"No, I'm checkin' you. Like, for real. Dang, *this is school*. *Not the block*. Ain't nobody checkin' for how thorough you supposed to be. This is the Dirty-Dirty and don't nobody wanna hear all that."

I lifted my eyes to the sky and said a quick prayer, 'cause Tasha didn't even realize she'd just put her life in my hands. I said, "He stepped to me! I don't know what kind of party you thought this was, but if you come for me, I finish you."

"Well you didn't finish him, 'cause he squashed you. And being that you were with me, now I been squashed too."

"He ain't squash nothin' over here. And, anyway, you're the one who said he was a square, a clown, and a dud. Basically a sucker."

"Okay, maybe I underestimated him. But, daaaaang! You didn't have to pop off like that."

"He came at me!"

"You started it...Look, if you gon' hang with me, I'ma

need you to chill with all that. Otherwise, I'ma have to kick you to the curb."

I gave her the screw face. "Puhlease, let's not forget that yesterday, you came lookin' for me. I didn't come checkin' for you. So don't get this confused. And trust, you'll never ever get the chance to kick me to the curb, 'cause right about now, I'm finish wit' you." I shoved my backpack farther up my shoulder and left her standin' there.

Trick.

13

If I Could Turn Back...

"I'm not stupid, if that's what you tryna find out," I said to the guidance counselor, Mrs. Brown, as she pointed to a metal, all-in-one student's desk and handed me the placement tests.

She leaned against her wooden bureau, covered with books, papers and framed pictures of kids, looked directly at me and smiled. "Yvette, I don't think you're stupid. Not at all. Why would I think that?"

"Why wouldn't you?" I looked over the blank answer sheet.

"I asked you first," she said.

True. "Well...'cause."

"Because what?"

"Just 'cause."

"Yvette, *because*"—Mrs. Brown stressed the word, like she wanted me to hear exactly the way the word should be said—"is not a complete thought. It's also not a complete sentence." She walked over to a rolling chair, pushed it next to me, and sat down. She tapped on my desk. "Put the paper down. Let's have a chat first."

Oh, here we go. "Look," I said, "before you even go there, I'm not in the mood to be social worked. I don't need nobody tryna get into my head. Tryna see if I know right from wrong. Tryna see if I'm retarded. Lookin' for love. Angry. Pissed off. Or just tryna see what's wrong wit' me. I don't need none of that. Just let me chill. Just let me live. All I want is to be here for a year, and then I'm out."

"I'm not trying to cramp your style or gag you with a spoon," Mrs. Brown said, soundin' crazy.

I didn't have a response for that, at least not one that wouldn't get me suspended. I picked up the test and said, "You got a pencil?"

Mrs. Brown chuckled. "Is that your way of saying I didn't sound fresh, or fly, or cool, or bad? Or ill? Or whatever it is you kids are saying these days?"

Don't say nothin'. Don't. Say. Nothin'.

She continued. "My son tells me to knock it off all the time."

"Good advice. 'Cause you sound like a straight corn-ball. Like you don't have no black in you at all." I looked in her caramel-colored face and smirked. When her eyes popped open wide and her broad nose flared in surprise, I wanted to slap myself in the mouth.

Dang.

By the time I count to three, she gon' put me out.

One . . .

Two...

Three...

"Yvette..."

I knew it. I stood up, slung my backpack over my shoulder, and said, "Already know."

"Know what? And where are you going?" She stood up and looked at me strangely.

"To the office."

"For what? I didn't ask you to leave. Sit back down."

I did as she asked, then waited for her to officially say *You gotta get the hell outta here!*

She didn't.

Instead, she retook her seat next to me and crossed her legs.

Before she could jump into some kind of lecture or try and read me, I said, "My fault. I wasn't tryna be disrespectful."

"I know that. It was actually kind of funny. Don't say it again. But I think we can let it slide this time."

"Oh...ai'ight. Thanks."

"You're welcome. And what's an *ai'ight*?"

This chick is pitiful. "It means it's all good. It's okay. Like, it's fine."

"Seems I have a lot of slang to learn." She smiled. "Now, let's get back to why you'd think, I'd think, you were stupid."

I shrugged. "Just 'cause...you know."

"Know what?"

"I know you saw my school records."

She nodded. "I did."

"Well, then, that's why. They basically said I was stupid. I went to school thirteen days last year. And in fifth grade, I stayed back."

She squinted. "Why only thirteen days?"

"I hated school. The only thing hittin' was the hallway, and after a while, hangin' in the hallway became played. Plus, I had a baby, and I ain't have nobody to keep her."

"What happened that you were retained in fifth grade?"

"My mother had just left me, so I spent most of the year cuttin' school and roamin' the streets lookin' for her."

"Did you find her?"

"No."

"How long has she been gone?"

"Five years."

"What do you think happened to her?"

I shrugged. "I know she ain't dead. I've had people to tell me they've seen her here and there."

"Do you still look for her?"

"Not really. I think about her, but I'm not searchin' the streets for her anymore."

"What do you think she's doing?"

"What fiends do—gettin' high. She'll show back up when she's on a sober stint or pregnant again."

Mrs. Brown paused, like she needed a moment to absorb all of that. She continued. "Okay, now tell me what part of everything you just told me do you think makes *you* look stupid?"

"I'm sixteen, in the ninth grade, when I should be a junior. How do you think I look?"

For the next few moments, we sat in thick silence. Then Mrs. Brown said, "I don't think you're stupid. I think you've been through a lot. I think the adults that didn't take care of you are stupid. But you, not at all. The real question is, what do you think of yourself?"

I picked up the tests, looked at the first question and didn't know the answer. "I don't know what I think. I just wanna get this over with."

14

How Can I Fail...?

"So what happens if I fail?" I asked Mrs. Brown, as I handed her the completed test.

"What happens if you succeed?" she asked me, smilin', placin' the test face down on her desk.

I couldn't answer that, 'cause I knew I'd failed.

I just knew it.

I could feel it.

Plus, I was the one who took the test; she didn't.

I read each question.

I answered 'em.

And no, I didn't feel stupid.

I felt...

...blank.

Empty.

School just wasn't for me.

Wasn't nothin' here gon' help me.

Gon' change me.

Gon' teach me.

I wasn't like these kids; even me and Tasha was different. They all acted like the only thing that mattered was a shawtie and a smile.

My life wasn't set up like that.

I was on my own.

I needed a job.

Money.

My own spot.

I ain't need to know why X plus Y equaled 23; that wasn't never gon' do nothin' for me. I ain't need to know why there was a Cold War between the United States and Russia. I had my own Cold War. I ain't need to read no stupid novels. All those words jumbled up on a page, tryin' to lure me into some fantasy...was just...whack.

And I hated those self-appointed shero and hero teachers, tryna save the world by spendin' an entire class talkin' about college.

Most of the time I wanted to stand up in the middle of the classroom and scream, *"Would you stop and think about what you sayin'?! I'm barely in high school. Now you think I should spend another four years in a classroom? For what? I ain't Denise Huxtable. My cracked-out mama ain't no lawyer and my cryptic daddy ain't no doctor. I don't live in a different world.*

"I live here. Where e'rybody I know parents is fiends. Where all the boys is either locked up, dead, clockin' drugs, runnin' drugs, runnin' from the cops, and if there's an exception, it's 'cause he got a wicked jump shot. And all the broads is lookin' for love and havin' babies. So don't nobody wanna hear about college. Ain't nobody got no money 'cause mostly e'rybody in here is hood rich or on welfare!"

But I would never say nothin'. I'd just walk out and kick it in the hallway.

"Ai'ight, Mrs. Brown," I said, shaking my thoughts. "Can I go to lunch now?"

All eyes was on me. From the moment I entered the buzzing and crowded cafeteria, walked over to the lunch counter, grabbed a grilled cheese and a Sunkist, to the moment I took an empty seat at the end of a packed table.

A few chicks stared and gave me the *you-can't-sit-with-us* face. But it was obvious a few of they dudes wanted me to stay.

I ignored all of 'em.

As long as they ain't start none, wouldn't be none.

I took a bite of my grilled cheese and pulled out my *Right On* magazine. Usually, leafin' through the pages and readin' about my favorite rappers was enough to entertain me.

But not today.

Today I felt like I was in Oz, tryin' to get home, but wasn't no home.

"Forget this." I slid my magazine into my backpack and just as I'd made up my mind that this was the end of the school day for me, a warm hand softly gripped my shoulder.

It was Tasha. "Hey, girl," she said like she'd forgotten that just this mornin', we was seconds away from tearin' up the concrete.

I ice-grilled her, 'cause seemed she'd lost her freakin' mind, touchin' and talkin' to me. I said, "*Hey, girl?* You gotta be trippin'. I don't know what part you missed, but we finished. I'm not messin' wit' you."

She smacked her gum. "Oh, you still mad?"

I blinked and turned around to completely face her. "Duh. Didn't we just have an argument?!"

"Yeah, but dang, girl, let that go."

"And why would I do that?!" I snapped.

"'Cause you too cute to stay mad, and me too. Plus, I said what I had to say, and so did you. When you walked away, I thought we had an understanding." She blew a pink bubble, popped it, and continued smackin' her gum.

"Chile, boo. Just this mornin' I was 'bout to wash you; now you want me to act like that never happened? For real, for real, you don't know me like that. *And didn't you say* you wanted to kick me to the curb? Trust and believe me, boo-boo, I will *never* give *nobody* the chance to try and play me!"

She stopped smackin'. "Look, cuz." Her Californian accent completely kicked in. "I'm not the one to *try* and play nobody, homie. Either I play you *all the way* or I don't. *So trust and believe me, boo-boo*, I wasn't tryna play you. I was tellin' you how I felt and that you needed to get a grip 'cause e'rybody ain't the enemy. You don't have to run up in nobody's neck around here."

"First of all, that joker came at me crazy!"

"Because you straight up stepped to him. I understand where you from, and where I'm from, you get done walkin' up on somebody you don't really know, but you ain't there no more! So what you need to do is take a chill pill and be sixteen."

"Girl, please, go sit down. Who you s'pose to be, Neighborhood Watch? The community counselor?! I don't need you to tell me nothin' about who I am, where I'm from, or where I'm at!"

"Would you lower you voice?" Tasha said, pointin' at

the gawkers whose eyeballs was glued to our conversation.

I looked around and they all quickly looked away. "Whatever," I said, turning back to Tasha and lowering my voice. "You see it your way, and I see it mine."

"It ain't even all that." Tasha grimaced.

"It is to me."

"Fine. Bump it. I'm tired of goin' back and forth with you. I see you like being a mad and miserable bitch."

"I'm glad you caught that; now stop sweatin' me."

"Ain't nobody sweating you."

"Good, don't."

"I won't." She rolled her eyes and walked away, leavin' me center stage.

I watched her as she sat at the lunch table directly across from me and greeted her friends.

I couldn't believe she came at me like that. *Gon' tell me I like bein' a mad and miserable bitch.* I don't know who she thinks she is!

And then she gon' say, I need to take a chill pill and learn how to be sixteen!

Like for real?

Word?

I have slapped people for sayin' less than that.

I really shoulda yoked her up and said, *Be sixteen? Trick, please! So what you think, bein' sixteen is some magic number where the only thing that matters is the gum you smackin' on? Is you crazy? You don't tell me how to do me! And just 'cause you caught up in this Never-Never Land don't mean I have to be. Check it, I'm the belle of this ball, and over here I got real dragons to slay. So you do your fairy tale your way, and I'ma get it how I live!* That's what I shoulda said, and if it wasn't for bein' tossed back on that pissy bus, carted back to jail, and losin' my baby, I'd run over there and shove it down her slutty, worn-out throat!

Twice today, she got off easy, but ain't no more chances, 'cause the next time her lips gon' be glossin' the concrete.

I looked over at the wall clock. Thirty long minutes 'til lunch was over.

I hated that I couldn't stop my eyes from wanderin' over to Tasha and her friends.

They better not be laughin' or talkin' about me.

One of Tasha's friends lifted her eyes and looked my way.

Oh these tricks wanna play. I know they over there doggin' my name! But I'ma put a end to this!

I got up outta my seat, rushed over to the table where Tasha and her friends sat and forced my way into the empty space next to Tasha. Then I said, "Somebody lookin' for me?"

Tasha paused mid-sentence; clearly I caught her off guard.

Yeah, now what! I dare you to say somethin' slick.

I pursed my lips, my eyes lettin' her know I didn't play games.

Tasha draped an unexpected arm over my shoulders and said, "They were just asking me who you were."

I knew they was talkin' about me.

Before I could brush Tasha's arm off of me and snap, she said, "I told them you just moved here and that we both lived with Aunty Glo."

I did my all to read her friends' eyes, wonderin' if they knew Aunty Glo equaled foster home. I waited for one of them to say it or hint at it.

They didn't.

Instead, their eyes invited me in.

"Welcome to Carver High! I'm Reesie, short for Cheresse." Reesie smiled, and her dime-sized dimples sank into her cheeks. Her skin was pale yellow with sunset red freckles lightly dusted over her face. She wore a white sweatshirt—with the word Fresh spray-painted across it in neon pink—and ripped jeans.

Tasha giggled as she introduced her other friend, who sat directly across from us and next to Reesie. "This is our girl Mother Earth."

Mother Earth had smooth, milk chocolate–colored skin and deep brown eyes framed with clear plastic gazelles. She looked stupid-fly rockin' her red, green, and black dashiki, black stir-up pants, Kari shell earrings, and a round leather medallion with the shape of Africa on it. She also wore a red leather kufi atop her long, black, box braids that spilled down her back.

Mother Earth snatched her gazelles off her face, then playfully swatted toward Tasha, and said, "Yvette, don't listen to T-Skee. My name is not Mother Earth; I'm Ebony."

"Hey, Reesie. Hey, Ebony," I said, feelin' awkward. "I'm Yvette."

Reesie pointed to my dark blue jeans with the words Fresh, Fly, and Bananas airbrushed in neon colors all over the front and back of them, and said, "Girl, them pants you got on is ill."

I smiled. "Thank you."

"Where you get 'em from?" Tasha asked.

"I made these a while ago. Well, I didn't make the jeans; I did the graffiti and the airbrush though."

"Word? Oh you got skills. I'ma need you to do my jeans like that!" Tasha said.

Reesie wiggled in her seat. "I got an idea! How about you make us all some. That way, when we go to the concert, we all look sick!"

"Yes!" they all agreed.

"You going, right?" Tasha pressed, taking a bite of her sandwich.

I wasn't sure if I should've said yes, no, or reminded her that I needed a babysitter. "I guess. Maybe so." I shrugged. "I'll let you know."

"Oh, you gotta go. Everybody gon' be there," Reesie insisted, opening a bag of salt-and-vinegar chips.

"She'll be there," Tasha said.

"Now, Yvette, where are you from?" Ebony asked. "'Cause with that accent, I know you're not from Norfolk."

"Nope. She's from Jersey," Tasha volunteered.

"Jersey?" Reesie's eyes popped open wide. "For real? Word?"

"Word," I confirmed.

Reesie carried on, "Y'all know my baby-love lives in Jersey. He said he's comin' down here to visit me soon."

"Lies," Ebony said, sippin' her soda.

"Don't be mad." Reesie popped her fingers. "You know I'm in love."

Tasha took a handful of chips from Reesie's bag and said, "Girl, stop. You are not in love; you are in dumb."

Ebony jumped in. "Plus, how you gon' love somebody you met on the party line and have never even seen?"

Reesie put her hands up. "Slow down, low down; don't judge my love. At least I'm not caught up in some Chinese Plug One wanna-be named Malik. And don't even get me started on you and yo' knock-off Bobby Brown, Mother Earth. Jheri curl, anyone?"

"You know you wrong for that." Ebony chuckled. "And he has an S-curl. There's a difference."

"And Malik is my soul mate—well, on Thursdays," Tasha insisted.

"And Jerelle is mine every day," Reesie said, then paused, "Well…on Mondays through Thursdays, 'cause on the weekends, I be getting it poppin' with Raheem. Feel me!" She and Tasha looked at each other, popped out of their seats, did a two second whop, and ended their dance with a fist bump.

"You know I feel you," Tasha said.

We all laughed.

"Yvette, you got a soul mate?" Ebony asked.

"Yep." I smiled.

"What's his name?" she asked.

"Big Daddy Kane, baby!"

Reesie snapped her fingers. "Girl, I'ma marry Big Daddy Kane!"

I gave her a pound. "Me, too!"

"Y'all nasty." Tasha frowned. "You gon' marry the same man?"

"Whatever," Reesie said. "You and Ebony love to act like y'all nuns. Let's not even bring up them twins y'all got mixed up." She paused and when they didn't respond, she carried on. "I ain't think y'all wanted none. 'Cause we all know y'all just mad that when we called the party line, I was the only one who walked away with a boo-freak, my Jerelle." She crossed her hands, pressin' them into her heart.

Ebony smirked. "He's probably an old nasty freak."

"You know he sounds young!" Reesie insisted.

"*Umm hmm.*" Tasha giggled. "A little too young, if you ask me."

"Well nobody asked either one of you, ma'am," Reesie said, as the bell rang. "Come on, Yvette, let's walk out together. Plus, I don't want you to be rude and bossy like Tasha and Ebony. Be the bomb like me."

15

Lucky Charm

I was all smiles 'til I walked into Mrs. Brown's office and looked into her face.

She sat at her desk, shook her head, and held my tests.

My heart sank to the bottom of my stomach, but I wasn't about to let Mrs. Brown know that.

"How was lunch, Yvette?" she asked, givin' me a fake smile.

"It was lunch. Like e'ry other meal."

"Would you cut the sarcasm?"

Silence.

"Now please have a seat."

I did as she asked.

She walked around her desk, leaned against the front of it, and looked directly at me. "What did you eat?"

I huffed. Pursed my lips. "Could you just get to the point?"

"Yvette..."

"Look, no disrespect, but I'm not no baby and I don't

have no sweet tooth, so whatever I had for lunch wasn't
sugarcoated. Please don't try and feed it to me now. I'm
just sayin', say what you gotta say, so I can be on my way."

"On your way where?"

"Outta here. If you think I'm 'bout to sit here in the
ninth grade *again*, with some li'l freshmen lookin' at me
like I belong in the thirteenth grade, you dead wrong. Not.
Gon'. Happen. I will figure it out. School ain't for e'rybody, 'cause it ain't never been for me."

Mrs. Brown placed the tests, face down, on the desk
where I sat, and said, "There are your tests; look them
over."

I ain't wanna look nothin' over. I just wanted to get up
outta there so the walls could stop closin' in on me. I ain't
touch the tests.

"Look them over," she demanded.

I sucked my teeth and did as she asked. Red ink was
marked up all over both tests. I rolled my eyes. *Whatever.*
I looked up at her. "Okay. I looked them over. It ain't no
more, or no less, than I expected. I failed. Okay, next."

"You have to stop using failure as a crutch."

Dear God. No. Not today. "Mrs. Brown, don't go there.
Like for real, I thought I would fail and I did. That's not
using failure as a crutch. That's keepin' it real. And I'm not
about to sit here and be lost in the dream clouds wit' you.
I'm sixteen, still in the ninth grade. When I'ma graduate?
When I'm twenty? What, me and my daughter gon' be in
school together? I ain't 'bout to sit here and play myself
like that. Nah."

"Yvette, so many things have happened to you that you
never expect to win. Winning is a state of mind. If you
want to win, then you have to start with believing that no

matter where you come from, the world is up for the taking and it can be yours."

She trippin, again. "Mrs. Brown, listen..."

"I don't want to listen. That's the problem; you're doing all the talking and you're not allowing anybody to offer you something different. You expected to fail, but guess what? You didn't."

"Didn't what?"

"Fail."

Just breathe. She don't mean no harm. And obviously she thinks this reverse psych is about to work. "I didn't fail, why? Because I took a chance and took the test. Because I'm now armed with everything I need to work on. Because I can be anything I want to be?" I said mockingly, whining. "Never mind that my mama's missin', my daddy's a blank line, and the only family I got is my baby. Never mind any of that 'cause I can be anything I wanna be, all 'cause people with college degrees, who have never lived my life, keep sayin' it to me?"

"You didn't fail because you're here. There are a million places you could've been, but you're here."

"It ain't that deep, Mrs. Brown. I don't have a choice. I'm just tryin' not to go back to jail and tryna keep my daughter outta foster care."

She shook her head. "So is that the answer to what you think of Yvette? A jailbird, with nothing and no one?"

Silence.

She continued. "Here's what I think of Yvette. I think you need to get out of the past and move forward because no amount of attitude, being pissed off, or feeling sorry for yourself will ever make your family the Brady Bunch. Yeah, your mother's somewhere out there. And your fa-

ther, too. But at this point, what is Yvette going to do for
Yvette? You can either make it happen for you and your
daughter or you can stay stuck in your parents' junk."

I wasn't about to stand here and argue with this lady.
The bell rang. "Okay. Now, can I leave?"

She looked up at the clock that hung above the door. It
was the end of the school day. "Yeah, you can leave," she
said, handing me a piece of paper.

"What's this?" I asked.

"Your junior class schedule."

"Junior? I don't get it."

"You're not a freshman. You're a junior."

"I passed the test?" I asked, shocked.

"With flying colors. Out of a hundred and fifty questions, you got five wrong. Had you actually taken the time
to read the tests over, instead of thinking you failed, then
you would've seen the *Congratulations, you passed!* written at the top of the paper."

I tried not to smile, but couldn't help it. "Mrs. Brown, I
just didn't expect . . . you know."

She nodded, like she understood what I was tryin' to
say. "I know. It's ai'ight. I got you."

I laughed and she did too.

"Thank you," I said.

"Thank me by being in class every day, not hanging out
in the hallway, and coming back to see me every Friday."

16

Express Yourself

"Look, Yvette. Listen. For real; no bullshit. Not today," I said to myself as I pressed my palms onto the bathroom's pink marbled vanity and leaned into the medicine cabinet's mirror. I locked eyes with my reflection and continued. "You cannot. Pop off. Today. Today, you gotta check yo'self."

I turned away from the mirror; then I remembered somethin'. "One more thing: You gotta go to all your classes. You gotta stay in *all of yo' classes* 'til the end."

I'ma try.

I shook my head. "No. You gotta do it."

I don't know how long I can do that.

"At least for a year."

You know how long a year is?

"Nothin', compared to being locked up."

But...a year stuck in space, wit' new people, new things, and new rules is a lot.

"Well, sometimes you just gotta do what you gotta do,

'cause it gotta be done. Period. And if you can't do it for
yourself,"

Then do it for Kamari.

"Yeah. Do it for Kamari."

I turned away from the mirror and headed out of the
bathroom, determined to get today right. I walked back
into my bedroom, where I'd left Kamari playin' on the
bed, and said, "Come on, Kamari; let's get you dressed before I go to...school..." I paused. My eyes scanned the
bed. No Kamari.

The kitchen. Suckin' down bacon grease.

Heading for the kitchen, I placed my hand on my door-
knob. That's when I spotted Kamari on the floor, beside
my dresser, gaspin' for air. Her round brown face was
sunken and pale purple; the whites of her eyes were dull
and wet with tears.

"What's wrong?!" I rushed over and snatched her off
the floor. "What's wrong?!" I felt Kamari's heart thunderin'
out of her chest, while mine cracked into jagged pieces.

She clutched my right arm, sinkin' her tiny nails into
my skin, strugglin' to breathe. She was chokin'...on
somethin'...but what? Her mouth hung open but nothin' was comin' out.

Panicked, I picked up Kamari and ran out of my room.
"Ms. Gloooo! Please! Help me! Help my baby!"

Ms. Glo, standin' in front of the stove, looked up.

Tasha at the table, jumped up and knocked over one of
the kitchen chairs to rush towards me.

Ms. Glo reached me first and ripped Kamari out of my
grip, shoved her arms around Kamari's tiny belly, made a
fist, and pushed into it.

Nothin'.

"Dammit, Kamari! Please! Breathe! Please!" I screamed. "I was only gone for a minute. A minute! Come on!"

Ms. Glo squeezed again.

Nothin'.

My baby was dead. I could see it. I could feel it. And it was my fault for leavin' her.

Dear God, please!

Please…

"Come on, baby!" Ms. Glo said, tears fallin' from her eyes.

My strength took flight and my legs became Jell-O. If somethin' happened to my baby, then that was it for me, too.

Wouldn't be nothin' to live for.

To fight for.

To see somethin' different for.

Seconds crept like hours.

"Ms. Glo, pleeeeeease," I begged as she squeezed until a penny flew from Kamari's small mouth and sailed across the room.

My baby swallowed a much-needed gulp of air, then burst into tears as she wrestled from Ms. Glo's grip and into my arms.

I fought with e'rything in me to hold back the tears that hammered against the backs of my eyes. But e'ry part of me wanted to collapse. E'rything I'd ever been through, ever seen…or didn't see…or no longer could see… crashed down on me in the middle of the yellow linoleum floor, while I held my baby and rocked back and forth.

Ms. Glo bent down on her knees, faced me and Kamari, and wrapped her arms around us, linkin' her fingers behind my back.

She rocked with me, placin' her cheek against mine.

"Yvette, you don't have to be tough all the time. It's okay to be scared."

Tears pounded, and I gave my all to swallow the stingin' lump in my throat, but it wouldn't go down. Instead it burned its way outta my eyes and sailed a shriekin' wail outta my mouth.

"Just let it go," Ms. Glo said, holdin' me tighter. "Let it go."

Through my tears, I heard myself babblin' and I kept tellin' myself to shut up, that I sounded crazy, but I couldn't stop talkin'. "I just feel so lost. I don't have anything, but my baby. And to think she almost died because of me."

Ms. Glo continued to rock with me. "Don't be so hard on yourself. That could've happened to anybody. And she didn't die. She's fine."

"I only left her for a second to go to the bathroom. If somethin' had happened to my baby, that woulda been it for me. She's all I have." I felt my tears soak through Ms. Glo's blouse.

I continued. "I'm just so...so tired. Tired of wonderin' why I'm here with nothin' and nobody. Tired of makin' the wrong turns while tryna find the right way. It's like e'ry breath I take got a noose in its way."

Ms. Glo didn't say anything; she just rocked with me.

I carried on. "And I'm tired of people tellin' me to stop bein' mad and to stop havin' an attitude, appreciate what I have. But what do I have but days, months, and years of the same shit? Nobody ever sees how hard it is to be me. And, yeah, I'm always mad and I got an attitude, but wouldn't you have one too? Now I'm here in a new place, a new space, new people, and e'rybody is lookin' at me like, 'you got a new chance. This is a new place; you can start again.' "

"You *can* start again," Ms. Glo said softly in a comforting whisper.

"But, Ms. Glo," I said, "do you know how many startin' agains I've had? E'ry time my mother left and came back, we was startin' again. I'm tired. I'm just tired. And I want out. I want out of feelin' like I gotta fight e'ry day. I just want a day where the only thing I gotta worry about is the gum I'm smackin' on."

Ms. Glo cupped my face. "Listen to me; you are only sixteen. Only sixteen. And you have to allow someone to get into your heart, into your space. Trust somebody to love you. To take care of you. That's what I'm here for. But you gotta let me in."

"I don't know how to do that. I don't even know where to start."

"Start by dropping the defense and simply be Yvette. That's it. Nothing more. Nothing less. Just simply be Yvette and everything else will fall into place."

17

Three Feet High and Rising...

I wasn't sure if I could do this.
Ten minutes into homeroom and I felt like bailin'.
There was no peace in here.
No quiet.
No courtyard.
No park benches.
No loosies.
No forties.
No Kamari.
No old heads passin' by to kick it.

Just twenty-plus high school juniors crammed into this one classroom, loud as hell. They only stopped talkin' long enough to say *Present* or *Here* when Mr. Harris, the teacher, did roll call.

Tasha, Reesie, Ebony, and me took up the middle row. I sat off to the far left, on the edge of my seat, my back pressed against the bulletin board. Tasha and her crew was pissed off 'cause they ain't get any tickets to the sold-out Dough E. Fresh concert.

The last row of the classroom was filled with dudes bangin' out rap beats on their desks with their pencils. Some of 'em was spittin' in a mini rap battle while a group of chicks was off to the side, dyin' to get noticed.

The front row was filled with kids sittin' at I-don't-want-my-mama-to-beat-my-ass-attention.

Meanwhile, I was just here, tryna shake my thoughts of where I really wanted to be.

"*Umm*, excuse me." Someone tapped my shoulder.

I turned around to the dude I'd nicknamed Whack-Skee, based on how corny he looked yesterday outside the school. Overalls must've been his uniform, 'cause he had on another pair, except today's was acid-wash green. That's when I noticed him sittin' next to Brooklyn.

My heart skipped two beats as Whack-Skee stuffed a note into my hand. "Yo, give this to Tasha for me." Quickly, I turned around, faced the front of the room and passed the note to Tasha.

"What's this?" she whispered.

I shrugged. "I don' know," I whispered back. "Ole boy in the back of the class asked me to give it to you."

Tasha swung around in her seat and looked at Whack-Skee. "Eww." She swung back around, tore open the note and said, "Look at this."

Yo Shawtie, I'm tryna see what's up with you. I like you. So circle yes or no if you like me too.

Tasha studied the note. "Chile, cheese. Boo, please. Next." She snapped her fingers. Then she circled, checked, and drew a cloud with her yellow highlighter over the word No.

And at the bottom of the note she wrote, Hell, no. Never. She folded it back up and said to me, "Pass this back to him."

I shook my head. "Girl, you really want me to give this to him?"

"Yes. I can't stand that boy and he knows it. If he was on fire, I wouldn't even spit on him to put it out."

"Okay, then," I said, and handed the note back to Whack-Skee.

He opened it. "Damn, homie!" erupted from the back row. E'rybody in the class turned around. Whack-Skee snatched the note back from Brooklyn.

"What is going on back there?" Mr. Harris asked, looking over his round, rimless glasses, peerin' at the back of the room.

"Nothing, Mr. Harris," Brooklyn said. "Sorry about that. I was just trying to get the notes for my next class." He topped off his lie with a smile. Then he looked at me and I quickly looked away.

Butterflies erupted. *Damn, he's fine.* I shook my head, hopin' he couldn't read my mind.

Mr. Harris tossed on his no-bullshit voice. "Everyone take out something to read. The bell will ring in the next few minutes and I don't want any more outbursts." He looked at one of the students in the front row. "Kaareema, I need you to come up here and see me, please."

Kaareema walked up to Mr. Harris and e'rybody returned to the exact same thing they were doin' at the top of the class.

"*Umm*, excuse me," came from behind me, again, accompanied by an annoying tap. I turned around and shot Whack-Skee a look. "What?!"

"Can you hand this to Tasha?"

I grabbed the note. "Here, Tasha. It's from your boyfriend."

"Don't play me." Tasha opened the note, blinked and ran her right palm over the paper to smooth out the wrinkles. Then she read it again. "Here." She handed it to me, bored. "Look at this."

It read: If you give me a chance at romance, then you'll see that we are meant to be. So would you like to be my date to the Dough E. Fresh concert? My cousin is a party promoter and he can get us in.

My eyes popped open wide.

"Does that say what I think it says?" she asked, takin' the note from my hand again. "Did he ask me to be his date to the Dough E. Fresh concert?"

"Yep. That's what it says."

"Lies," she said.

"You don't believe him?"

"Hell, no. Li'l Herman ain't got no juice like that."

Li'l Herman?

My mouth dropped open.

Tasha pushed up my chin. "I know, gross. Now back to the matter at hand. What should I write back? 'Die Slow?'"

"No. You gotta write more than that." I snatched the note from her, picked up my pen, and wrote, The only way I'ma go is if you get my girls in. If you can't get the four of us in, then no, die slow. We smirked and shot each other a high five.

The bell rang and e'rybody popped out of their seats like toast, bumrushin' toward the door. Whack-Skee lollygagged in the back of the room, his desperate gaze dug into Tasha, as we walked toward him. She handed him the note and as we walked out and into the hallway, Brooklyn looked directly at me and said, "So you just gon' keep bein' rude? What? You can't speak?"

Screech. Stop the press. Wait a minute. Pause. "*What?*" I looked at Tasha. "I don't know who he's talkin' to."

"You." She popped her lips. "Yup. You would be home-girl of the hour. *Now keep it cute.*"

I was too tongue-tied to keep it cute and my unexpected brain freeze wouldn't let me think of anything quick to say.

So instead, I looked back at Tasha. "Like *I said*, I don't know who he's talkin' to." And I walked away, leavin' e'rybody standin' there, while I prayed—all the way to my locker—that the jumpin' butterflies in my stomach didn't force the jelly in my knees to give way.

By the time I made it to my locker, my heart was in full panic mode and the butterflies in my stomach fluttered like crazy.

Five.

Four.

Three.

Breathe.

Okay...okay...I got it.

It's all good.

"Yo', you got a minute?" fell over my shoulder.

Oh, hell no!

I froze.

Brooklyn.

Again.

Oh. My. God.

Breathe.

Breathe.

I slammed my locker shut and whipped around, in full screw-face, hoping my eyes didn't soften as they swept over him. His smooth brown frame was dressed in a cream and hunter green leather Guess jacket; a light green tee shirt, with the Guess logo in the center of it. His deep blue Levi jeans hung slightly off his waist, givin' sneak peaks of the white boxers he wore beneath his pants.

I forced myself to suck my teeth. "Do I have a minute? Boy, please. What? You don't have enough time of your own, now you need some of mine? Hell, no. Now get off my tip."

Why did I say that?

Whyyyyy did I say that?

Brooklyn took two steps toward me, then one more into my personal space; I was pleasantly trapped and my back was pressed against my locker.

His hot breath was the essence of sweet butterscotch, as he hooked his russet brown eyes into mine, radiatin' a strength that I'd never experienced and didn't quite understand. Desperately, I wanted to lift one of my hands and wave it over my face like a fan.

"You know what?" he said. "You need to learn to shut up sometimes."

"Or what?" I shoved a hand up on my hip.

"Check it; I'm not..." He paused. Pulled in a deep breath. Pushed it out. "So you really wanna do this another day?"

"Do what?"

"Beef. Or you gon' let me apologize and get this over with?"

Apologize? Was he serious?

"Yeah, apologize," he said, like he'd read my mind.

This was too good to be true. "And what? Do you want your dollar back?"

"Look, this is not about a dollar. This is about me call- ing you a ho. And how bad I felt for saying that."

Keep it cute raced through my mind, as I searched for somethin' to say. "Okay..." I hesitated. "Well...I guess I need to apologize to you, too."

He raised a brow. "You guess? Yo, if you was a li'l bigger, you would've body-slammed me."

I shook my head. "Size doesn't matter to me. Trust, if I wanted to body-slam you, ya boys woulda been standin' over you sayin', 'Down goes Frazier!'"

He laughed. And, oh, what a cute laugh!

I continued. "About yesterday, though, my bad. I ain't have to pop off like that. I hope you can accept my apology."

"Of course," he said.

Is he blushin'?

Is he?

Oh my God, am I blushin'?

"So does this mean we can start again?" he asked, as the late bell rang.

"I guess." *Am I still blushin'?*

"You guessing again? Pretty girls should always be sure."

Now I had a full on grin...I couldn't help it. And for once, I didn't want to. "I'm sure; let's start again." I held out my fist for a pound and instantly regretted it. Did girls give guys pounds or did givin' pounds make me one of the guys, in his eyes?

Unsure, I almost tucked my fist back in, until he took his fist, completed the pound and said, "That's wassup. I'm Brooklyn."

"Hi, Brooklyn," I said, and some dumb giggle slipped out. "Yvette."

"Yvette." He softly flicked my chin with the length of his index finger. "I like that. Maybe we can catch up after class." He took a step back.

"Yeah, maybe."

18

Me, Myself, and I

"Heifer!" Tasha flopped down in the center of my bed, tossin' her clear jelly backpack on the floor. "Why'd you rush home so fast after your last class? I was looking for you. *And* Brooklyn"—she paused—"was looking for you too." She sat Indian-style with one elbow pressed into her thigh, her hand tucked under her chin. Her eyes demanded that I have an acceptable explanation. She blinked. "I'm listening."

I sat on my bed with my back against the white iron headboard, clutchin' Kamari's pink Care Bear to my chest. "'Cause."

"'Cause what?"

"You was takin' too long and I couldn't wait. I had to get home."

"Lies. Aunty Glo and Kamari are not even here. You could've waited for me."

"How would I know they wouldn't be home?"

Tasha twisted her lips.

"Okay, look," I said, "tomorrow, I'll wait. Now can we drop it?"

"*Umm-hmm*. Now on to Brooklyn. I saw him follow you to your locker. But just as I was about to go behind y'all and see what was goin' on, Li'l Herman called me a cock-blocker."

"No, he didn't!"

"Yes, he did." She snapped her fingers. "And you know me. So you know he got checked."

"Dang. Did you call off your date?"

"Heck, no. I ain't stupid. After I told him off, I smiled and said, 'I'll see you tomorrow, pumpkin.'"

I snickered. "Both y'all sick. And twisted."

"So what's up with you and Brooklyn? 'Cause Reesie told me that she was passin' by and saw you and Brooklyn kissing. And I was like 'Whaaaaaat?' And Ebony was like, 'Stop playin', yo.' Then Reesie swore on her dead grand-mamma that she was tellin' the truth. But that don't mean nothin', 'cause Reesie's Grandmamma was a lady of the night, which means that swearin' on her grave don't mean a thing. So I figured when I got home I'd go straight to source. Now did you kiss or is Reesie lyin' again?"

"No, we didn't kiss. Reesie know she goin' to hell with gasoline drawls on." I continued. "But he did flick my chin. Well, kind of, I guess."

"He did what? And what do you mean kind of? You guess? That's like bein' a li'l pregnant. Is the piss hot or not?! Now would you tell me what happened before I burst!"

This chick has got to be the nosiest person that I know. "Yes, he flicked my chin," I said.

"Flicked it, like how? Like this?" She inched over toward me and gently ran her whole hand under my chin. "Or like this?" She made a closed fist and softly nudged the bottom of my right cheek.

"Like this." I took my index finger and swept it under her chin.

"*Ouleee weee*, baby! Yes!" she squealed, fallin' back on the bed and kickin' her legs in the air. A few seconds after her excited fit, she resumed her original position, then said, "I know your moisture meter was off the rack! You know that means he wanna bone."

All I could do was shake my head and fall out laughin'. This trick was really crazy. "You know you're nasty, right? A straight freak."

"Whatever. Freaks are God's children too. And you still didn't answer my question."

"I don't have an answer for that. Plus, he'd have to do a whole lot more than flick my chin to get some. I'm not that easy. And besides, I'm just tryna get things together for me and my baby. I don't have time for boys."

Tasha looked at me strangely. "So what you're sayin' is, you've gone from dragging some heifer off the bus and beating her down, to now tryna be like Jesus. That's what you're telling me?"

"I am not tryna be like Jesus."

"Then what's the problem? How can you *not* have time for boys? Unless you have time for girls." She closed one eye and squinted with the other.

"You have lost your mind."

"I'm just asking. It's no judgment over here, 'cause sometimes I wonder about Ebony. So you can tell me anything."

"Not that I have to explain myself, but just so you're clear, I like boys. I just don't have time for any right now."

"Why not? What else do you have to do?"

"I have plenty to do. I have a baby, remember?"

"That's what I'm saying. So puhlease stop acting like a saint, 'cause at some point, them panties hit the carpet."

"This is not about my panties hittin' the carpet."

"Then what is it?" she pressed.

"Brooklyn is different. I've never messed wit' anyone like him before."

"First time for everything."

"Plus, I don't even think he likes me for real. I think he sees me like"—I snapped my fingers—"a possible homie."

Tasha curled her upper lip. "So you think he followed you to your locker 'cause it's what, Wednesday? Chile, please."

"Maybe he followed me 'cause he's a nice guy who wanted to apologize for callin' me outta my name."

"He ain't that dang nice. He apologized and he followed you down the hall because he knows you're pretty and he likes you. Hello." She waved a finger before my eyes. "This is how it goes. Boys are like hound dogs. They sniff out and piss up their territory; everybody knows this."

"What's with you and all this piss? That's so disgusting."

"Don't change the subject. He likes you."

"Tasha, unlike you, guys do not be checkin' for me like that. When I walk into a room, I swear they see e'ry girl but me."

Tasha shook her head. "That's not true. Did you not see how many dudes were sweatin' you today in school?"

"No, I didn't. Especially since all those phantom dudes didn't say nothin'."

Tasha stared, then said, "Can I ask you a question?"

"Now you need permission?"

"Not really. So, okay, let me ask you this: When's the last time you went on a date?"

"A date?"

"Yeah, like the movies, the arcade, the mall, hangin' out in the park and kicking it with a dude."

"Umm." I snapped my fingers. "Never."

"I'm serious," she said.

"I am too."

"Wait... What? So you've never been on a date before? What about Kamari's father?"

"Girl, please. All he could offer me was something to get high with. That's it. I don't even know how I fell for him," I said, disgusted.

"Get high? You mean smoke weed?"

I paused, and drifted into an unexpected vision of me and Flip free-basin' rock. "Sometimes weed. Sometimes a little more than weed."

I could tell Tasha didn't know what to say, so I carried on. "I only got high with him a few times. I never liked the way it made me feel. Plus, I ain't wanna end up doin' to Kamari what my mother did to me, so I stopped."

"Just like that?"

"I ain't have a choice. I wasn't about to be nobody's junkie."

"Where's Kamari's father now?"

"In Jersey."

"Duh. I figured that. But I mean, what is he doin'?"

"I guess whatever old fiends do."

"Old?" She frowned. "Like how old?"

"Like thirty."

"Dang, he's old as hell."

"Tasha, you should know that when you're out there in

the street, on yo' own, and doin' yo' own thing, age ain't nothin' but a number. He was just somebody who told me I was pretty and gave me some attention."

"It still wasn't right. He was too old to be messin' with you."

I shrugged. "It don't have to be right to be real. So no, I've never gone on any dates. I've never had a boyfriend. And I've never had any dudes tryna get with me, other than an old fiend on the street. And that's why today I jetted right after school, 'cause I didn't know what to say to Brooklyn, and I wasn't sure if he was really checkin' for me anyway."

Tasha scooted to my right side and draped an arm over my shoulders. "Brooklyn's checkin' for you. Trust me."

Silence seemed to be the only thing that could fill this moment, but a few minutes into it, Tasha hopped off the bed. "Dang, I almost forgot! Ebony and Reesie are outside."

I blinked. "All this time?"

"Yeah. I ain't wanna just bring 'em in here and bumrush you wit' no company. I had to see what kind of mood yo' lightswitchin' behind was in."

"Whatever." I chuckled and scooted off the bed. "Let's go outside."

"Bet. But, *umm*," she hesitated.

"What?"

She twirled a lone end of her hair. "It, *umm*, might be a few other kids from school outside too."

"Why?"

Tasha handed me a handmade business card. It read, "For customized denim with personalized New York subway style graffiti, come see Vette-B."

I was completely confused. I read the card again. "Come see Vette-B? Who is that?"

Tasha smiled. "*Umm*, yeah, about that. Vette-B would be you."

"What the hell?!" *Was she crazy?* "Are you crazy? First of all, who told you to do this? Second of all, Vette-B? Where'd the B come from? My last name is Simmons. And third, I'm from New Jersey, not New York."

"I know, but Vette-B sounds dope. We couldn't say Vette-S; how whack is that? And I know you're from New Jersey, but more people know where New York is at."

"It's somethin' wrong with you. I'm convinced."

"Is there something else you have to do? No." She answered her own question. "And besides, it's already a few people waiting outside for you. Cheddar in hand."

"Cheddar? Like money?" My eyes popped open wide.

"No, like cheese. Of course like money!"

"*Soooo* not only did you go around tellin' people that I would air-brush their denim, you charged 'em."

"This is 1989; ain't nothin' free, girl. Do you know what this could mean for us?"

"Us?"

"Yeah; we're business partners. I manage you. And Reese and Ebony are the hype crew. And you gon' be the designer and the secretary, keep the orders straight. Now check it, this is how it all started. When me and Reesie was in algebra, this girl, Pam, walked over and said to me, 'I saw you with this new girl yesterday, blahzay-blahzay. Her pants was fresh, yada-yada. Do you know where she got 'em from?' And Reese was like, 'Yop. We sure do. Give us a minute and after school we'll have our card for you.'"

"Our?"

"Our. Us. Now let me finish."

"Go 'head."

"So, me, Reesie, and Ebony discussed it and decided that the idea of having our own clothing business was fresh. And we wanted to run all this past you, after school, and get your thoughts. But when we couldn't find you, we took it upon ourselves to make it happen, and the rest is Vette-B graffiti-wear history. Now, Vette-B, we need to go. It's bad business to keep our customers waiting."

"And where we gon' get all this paint from?" I asked.

"Li'l Herman. His daddy owns a hardware store. So I told him if you expect me to chill witchu, then you need to get this paint for me."

"Did he?"

"He's already *outsiiiide*! So we in the *hoooooouse*, baby! Now come on!" Tasha opened my bedroom door and I walked behind her, in disbelief that any of this was happening.

"How many people, besides Ebony and Reesie, are outside?" I asked.

"Not many." Tasha pushed open the screen door leading to the porch. She said, "Like two."

I stepped onto the porch and there was a line of kids halfway down the block. "You mean like twenty-two."

"Stop exaggerating. It's like twenty."

My eyes scanned the line of smilin' teens, all with jeans tucked in the creases of their arms. "All I know is that if Ms. Glo comes home before these people leave, she gon' kick *yo'* behind. Not mine."

19

New Jack Swinga

Cruisin' down the street in my '64! Blasted from Li'l Herman's boom box as he lined up ten cans of multi-colored paint across Ms. Glo's bottom step. Tasha and Reesie laid two white sheets across the lawn, while me and Ebony hung a piece of cardboard from the wooden porch railing.

A steady line of kids, with jeans, tee shirts, and denim jackets in hand, snaked down the block. No one seemed to mind waitin', especially since there was a block party started. A group of kids in windbreaker suits break danced and did the whop in the street and on the sidewalk; and another group was shootin' dice at the bottom of the driveway.

Tasha and Reesie walked over to me and Ebony.

"We 'bout to make mad loot, homie!" Tasha said, her Californian accent in overdrive. "I promise you, blood, e'rybody gonna want Vette-B's airbrush."

"Word up!" Reesie slapped Tasha a high five.

"Yooo, this was the dopest idea yet, Tasha," Ebony said.

"Dope idea or not," I said, "I just hope we can pull it off before Ms. Glo comes home."

"Girl, Ms. Glo is at prayer meeting," Tasha insisted. "And those meetings last at least three, four hours."

"You sure?" I said. "Remember, she has Kamari with her."

"Exactly. So they may be gone even longer than that. I'm sure those old ladies are eating Kamari up. Believe me, Aunty Glo will not be coming home any time soon."

"But what happens if she does?" I pressed.

"Then I'll handle it. I got Aunty Glo wrapped around my finger. Trust."

"I hope so," I said. "'Cause your fingers are not that long, so let's hope she hasn't slipped off."

"Okay, pissy Patty, you sending my high to hell. Chill. Now everything is all set up, so, if it's okay with you, can we start calling these people over here so we can get this money?"

My eyes scanned the block; half of Norfolk seemed to be out here. The last time I'd seen this many people in one place, it was tax time in Da Bricks and e'rybody was coppin'. My gut was on edge, but I was trying my best to loosen up. I pushed a smile onto my face and said, "Let's get it!"

Tasha spun around toward the crowd. "Time to get hooked up! Vette-B is red'ta go. So step up, step up! Where ya dollars at?"

"Hey." The first person, one of the girls who lived down the street, walked up to me. "We go to the same school and I thought those pants you had on was fly." She handed me a pair of jeans and a tee shirt. "So I wanted you to put my name, my boyfriend's name, my cousin's baby's name, my mama's name, and..."

"That's enough," Tasha said. "We don't have all night."

Screeeeeeeech!

Boom!

Ms. Glo.

Everybody froze.

"What in the?!" Ms. Glo yelled, as she hopped out of her dark brown sedan, which I could've sworn had popped a wheelie and landed lopsided on the curb. "Why are all these kids lined up outside of my house?" she said to no one in particular, her eyes takin' in the crowd. She stomped over to the driveway. "I know you weren't shootin' dice on my property!" She slapped both hands on her hips, looked up toward the heavens, then slowly lowered her eyes over the crowd. "Everybody go home!"

I looked at Tasha. "Oh, she gon' be gone for three, four hours. I got her wrapped around my finger."

"Shut up," Tasha mumbled.

"That's what I should've told you when you told me this dumb idea—to shut the hell up!"

Ms. Glo stormed onto the lawn. "And y'all got my clean white sheets out here on the ground?! I just washed them sheets! Tasha, Yvette, you two have serious explaining to do!" Ms. Glo looked over at Reesie and Ebony. "By the time I count to three, you'd better be gone. One," she said, "three!"

Reesie and Ebony took off running down the street. Ms. Glo turned back toward the crowd. "I said *take y'all behinds home!*"

All the kids scattered except me, Tasha, and Li'l Herman.

"Li'l Herman," Ms. Glo said, "you don't understand English? Didn't I say leave? I tell you what, if you don't get yo' thieving behind outta here, I'ma call your daddy and tell 'em you have stolen the paint out of his store again!"

"Okay, I gotta go," Li'l Herman said. "I'll come back for the paint."

"Wait, Ms. Glo," Tasha said, embarrassed.

"Wait for what? For you to ask my permission if you can have a party on my front lawn? Never!"

"We weren't havin' a party," Tasha swore.

Ms. Glo carried on. "Now I gotta explain this to the pastor and the sisters from the church! They came over here for a little peace, quiet, and some tea, and now they are scared out of their damn minds!" She pointed to her car where two old women, whose eyes were popped out like a deer's, sat. The only one who didn't appear to be scared was Kamari, and that's 'cause she was sleeping.

"Aunty Glo, just let me explain," Tasha carried on. "See, what had happened was, *umm*, Vette-B."

"Who is Vette-B?" Ms. Glo looked at me.

"Don't look at me. Ask Tasha," I said.

"It's Yvette's stage name," Tasha answered.

I could've kicked Tasha dead in her throat.

"Stage!" Ms. Glo yelled. "What the heck kind of party was y'all having?!"

"No! Chill, Aunty Glo!" Tasha said. "That's not what I meant!"

"I know dang well you're not yellin' at me!"

Seeing that Tasha's foot was pretty much cloggin' her throat, I said, "Ms. Glo, can I please explain?"

She hesitated, then said, "I'm listening."

"First, Tasha is out of control. And second, this was her idea."

"Snitch," Tasha mumbled, but I let her get that.

I continued, "She meant well, though. See, I do this thing called air-brushing. It's like drawing with paint. E'rybody's rockin' it on their clothes. So all the kids at school wanted me to design somethin' for them. And that's why they were all here."

Ms. Glo took in three deep breaths before she said anything. "The next time you two get another bright idea like this and don't ask me first, all the li'l rules of what I can and cannot do to you will go out the window, and I'ma get me a switch and tear y'all asses up. And I mean that." She marched over to her car and opened the passenger side door. "Come on, Sisters, it's safe now." Then she walked around to the other side and lifted a sleeping Kamari out of the car and on to her shoulder. "I'm going to lay this baby down and reassure my sisters that I am not running a crack house." She looked over at me and Tasha. "You two clean up this mess!"

"Well, Vette-B," Tasha said, after e'rybody had gone inside. "I guess your business is officially black history."

20

Every Little Step...

"Time to go night-night," I said to Kamari, who played on the floor as I lay down on the bed and patted the center of it.

Kamari shook her head no. "Not yet, Mommy." Her loose curls bounced with every word.

"But it's late," I said, as if I could really convince her that there was a difference in it now being ten o'clock at night and not ten o'clock in the morning. "And I have school tomorrow."

Kamari hugged her Care Bear and rocked it in her arms. "Cheer Bear wanna play."

I nodded. "Okay, go on and play."

"Yay!" she said, then sang the *Sesame Street* song to her bear. "Can you tell me how to get..."

I propped two pillows behind my back and stared at Kamari, wonderin' if she remembered us sittin' in Da Bricks' courtyard, dreamin'. Dreamin' about what she could be when she grew up. How I was not gon' let her have a life like mine. She was gon' have a chance to be anything she wanted to be.

I wondered if she remembered being in foster care when I was in jail.

Janette had said the people were nice to her and wanted to keep her.

I hated her for telling me that, and I hated the foster parents even more.

"I ain't never losin' you again. You hear me, Kamari."

She didn't even turn around.

"I love you, Kamari, and I'll do anything for you."

Kamari looked up at me and smiled, then continued singing to her bear.

I continued with our one-sided conversation. "Today was a pretty okay day. I mean, it started out crazy. I was so scared when you had that penny in your mouth. And I know you were too. No more money in your mouth, Kamari. No more. You hear me?"

"How to get to Sesame Streeeeet..." Kamari continued to sing.

"I'll take that as a yes. And I'ma make sure there's no money left on the floor. And Tasha with that Vette-B business." I laughed. "Yo, that chick is off her rocker. But I like her. She's cool. And Ms. Glo..."

I fell silent and looked around the room. The walls were covered in beige wallpaper with the same small pink daisies that were on the sheets and the comforter.

Two small windows were to the right of the bed, both covered with white pull-down shades, framed by light pink lace curtains. On the floor was burgundy carpet. There was a nightstand on each side of the bed and a mirrored dresser against the wall, by the door.

I guess I could say the room was the pretty.

I continued. "I feel bad for the way I treated Ms. Glo when we first got here. She didn't deserve that. And then today with the Vette-B disaster. I knew that was a bad idea. I mean, I don't mind airbrushin', but all those people lined up like that made this place look like a trap house. Thank God the cops ain't roll up."

I fell silent again and took in the room once more.

"I'ma make this place work. I promise we're gon' have a good year and I'm not gon' mess it up. I'ma find a way to float above it all. No worries. No pain. And no thinkin' about what tomorrow may bring."

"Mommy," Kamari said, climbing onto the bed. "Time to go night-night."

"Yeah, time to go night-night." I smiled, reached over on the nightstand and turned the light off.

21

My Prerogative

"Good morning, class," Mr. Harris said as we all filed into homeroom and took our self-assigned seats.

"Yo," Reesie said to me and Tasha in a concerned whisper. "I was so worried I wasn't gon' see y'all this morning."

"Why?" I frowned, slightly concerned about what would come out of her mouth.

"'Cause," Reesie carried on. "After the way Ms. Glo lost it, I just knew y'all was gon' wake up dead this morning. I had my black dress ironed and my mama's brown liquor ready to be poured out."

"First of all, how do you wake up dead?" Ebony said.

Reesie smacked her lips. "The same way you got smart with your mother, and I watched her knock you clean into the next week."

Ebony said, "You talk too much."

"That's the same thing yo' mama told you before sent you into the future."

"Hey, Tasha," came from behind us. Tasha rolled her eyes to the ceiling, then turned around. "Hey, Li'l Herman."

"Y'all ai'ight?" he asked.

"We're fine." Tasha popped her eyes wide, and wiggled her neck, clearly aggravated. "Thank you."

"That's wassup." He nodded. "Glad to hear that. So"— he flipped up the collar of his green Izod shirt—"maybe, ah, we can kick it real soon."

"We just did," Tasha answered and turned back around in her seat.

"Why are you bein' so mean to him?" I asked.

"I'm not being mean. Didn't I tell you that boys were like hound dogs? I'm sending him on a chase."

Tasha slapped Reesie a high five and said, "After all, if a dog want a bone, then he got to hunt for it."

"Speakin' of dogs on the hunt," Ebony said, "Reesie told us that she saw you and Brooklyn gettin' busy at your locker."

"I didn't say that. I said they were kissing," Reesie insisted.

"Both of y'all loud and wrong," I said. "He only flicked my chin. That's it."

"*Umm hmm,*" Reesie said. "Y'all was awfully close."

"So?" I shrugged.

"What do you mean, so?" Ebony asked. "It's obvious that you like him, so what's up with that?"

"That's what I wanna know," Reesie said. "So are you trying to get with him or what?"

"No," I said as the bell rang and e'rybody popped out of their seats. "I am not even thinking about him like that. He's cute and all, but that's it. So if any of you three want him, he's yours for the takin'." I slung my backpack over my shoulder and swallowed my smile, as I shot Brooklyn a quick wave and continued on to my next class.

2:30 p.m.

"Yo, slow up."

I didn't have to turn around to know that was Brooklyn. I felt his hand grab mine. "Hey, wassup?"

I did my best to fake surprise. I jumped. Pushed out a breath, then said, "You scared me."

"I didn't mean to scare you, Love," Brooklyn said, as he boldly lifted my cup of soda out of my hand. "Scaring you is the last thing I'd want to do." He took a loud sip from my cup and came up empty.

"Dang, you drank all of it." He tossed the cup into the trash.

"It was my soda." I crossed my arms over my chest.

"But I wanted some."

"You wanted some too late."

"I'd better be on time for the next round."

"I guess."

"Guessing again?"

I stared at him and drifted into an unexpected thought of how it would feel to kiss him. Heated? Soft? Wet? Extra wet?

"So where are you on your way to?" he asked.

"Home," I lied. I was actually waiting around for Tasha, like I'd promised her yesterday that I would do. But when I saw Brooklyn come out of the school, I turned the other way and started walking through the parking lot.

"Where do you live?" he asked, but I couldn't answer him. I was too busy admiring how good he looked in his red Bermuda Kango and black Levi's denim suit. "Bricks," he called.

I blinked.

"Bricks," he repeated. "You hear me?"

"Huh? What? What did you call me?"

He smiled. "Bricks."

"Bricks?" *What the hell? First Vette-B and now Bricks.* "It's Yvette."

"I know that. But you're little and tough, so you remind me of a brick."

Little? Tough? A brick? What the heck kind of description and nickname is that? Bricks are not cute. Or pretty. They are chipped up and used. Dang, he could've called me Hot-to-Trot, Brown Sugar, Kitten, Kissy Face, a million other sexy things, but he wanna call me Bricks; well, damn.

"If you don't like it, I'll drop it. I just thought it was kind of fly, like you," he said.

Awww. It is kind of cute. "I think I like that. It's cool. Plus, I'm from Brick City."

"Newark?" he asked, shocked.

"Yeah, why?" I cocked my neck to the side. "You got an issue with Jersey or something?"

"No disrespect. I didn't mean it like that. It's just that, when Tasha handed out those Vette-B cards, she told everybody you were from New York."

"Don't listen to Tasha."

"Ai'ight." He laughed as he leaned against the hood of a two-door, silver Chevette, sliding his hands in his pockets.

Like a magnet I took two steps toward him. Then I caught myself and took three back. He reached for my hand and pulled me close. "Now tell me your address."

"You're awfully pressed about that," I said, playfully.

"What? You think I'ma stalk you?" He tucked my hair behind my ears.

"I don't know you like that. You might."

He gave me a crooked grin. "Yeah, I might."

An unexpected giggle slipped out.

He continued, "Nah, Bricks, I'm not gon' stalk you. I wanted to give you a ride home; that's all. Chill with you for a minute."

I smiled. "I guess we can arrange that. I live the same place Tasha does."

His eyes lit up. "That's across the street from me."

"Oh, hold up!" Some tall chick, with her neck twisted and her hair swingin' came out of nowhere and walked up on us. "Brooklyn, who is this?"

"You'd better back up." He placed his hands on my waist, and moved me to the side. He stood up.

The girl flared her hands in the air. "This is why I can't get you on the phone! You trippin' on me for this stupid trick. For this ho! What you looking at?" She huffed and attempted to run up on me.

Brooklyn pushed her back.

Wait, what just happened here? "Come again?" I said. "Trick? Ho? Stupid? I don't know what time you think it is, but don't get my short ass twisted."

"Let her go!" the girl yelled.

I did my best to move around Brooklyn, but couldn't. "Yo, calm down," Brooklyn pleaded.

"Ain't no calm down," I went on, my eyes daring the girl to say another word to me. "Trust, somewhere in this world is a chick laid up with her face peeled open for doin' less than what you just did. So I won't hesitate,

Black, to snatch your cranium back. Therefore, I advise
you to keep this between you and your boyfriend."

"Chill," Brooklyn said.

I continued. "You better tell ya broad that, 'cause I ain't
chillin' 'til I'm done. I don't know how y'all do it down
here, but homegirl ain't about to run up on me. I'm not
no punk. Now check it. You can hash this out with him
now, or after he takes me home. But either way, you need
to keep anything havin' to do with me outta ya mouth!
And that's real."

"Would you chill?" Brooklyn said, opening his car door.
"Just get in. I got this."

"You better get it before I end it."

"I said get in," he demanded.

Everything in me wanted to hook off on this trick, but I
knew she wasn't worth it. So I listened to Brooklyn and
got in the car.

I cracked the window though. I had to hear anything
else this skeezer had to say.

"Alesha, what's yo' problem, yo?" Brooklyn said. "How
many times we gotta go through this? How many times I
gotta tell you to step off. I'm done with you. We're finished."

"I ain't goin' nowhere!" Alesha said, lookin' stupid.

Brooklyn shook his head. "Know what, you don't have
to." He walked around to the driver's side of the car and
got in.

She tried to snatch the door open. "You better let me
in! You better not go nowhere, Brooklyn!"

He started the engine.

She jumped in front of the car.

"Watch me." He jerked the gear in reverse.

"Dumb ho!" I yelled out the window, as he backed up.

"Watch your mouth," Brooklyn said, as he took off for the street. "I told you I had it."

"Look, I was not about to let that trick come for my neck."

"I wouldn't have let that happen. So it was no need for you to lose your cool; plus, you're too pretty for that," he said.

"Is that what you tell all the girls? When she runs up and attacks them?"

"It ain't even like that, and why are you worried about all the girls when the only one I'm worried about is you."

Silence.

Did he just say that?

"Don't get quiet on me now," he said.

"I'm not. I'm just waiting for you to get to the part where you explain to me what's up with you and homegirl from the parking lot."

"It's nothing up."

"Apparently, she thinks you're her boyfriend."

"She knows I'm not her boyfriend," he said, stopping at a red light.

"So y'all broke up?"

The light turned green and he took off. "Yeah. About two months ago."

"She's pyscho. That's the line you wanna feed me? You had to do something to send her crazy."

He smirked, as he turned the corner. "I didn't do anything. We just grew apart, and she's having a hard time accepting that. So I guess when she saw me with you, she lost it."

"How long were you together?"

"About six months."

"You loved her?"

"I liked her. Now enough of that. I want to talk about something else."

"Like what?"

"Like me and you and when you're going to let me take you out." He pulled up and parked in front of Ms. Glo's house.

Breathe.

Breathe.

Chill.

Relax.

"Thank you for the ride, but I don't think we should go out."

He arched a brow. "Why not?"

"Because." And that's all I said before I hopped out the car and ran up the steps.

I opened the screen door, rushed in, and of course Tasha was peekin' out the window.

"Heifer," she said, following me to my room, "you better start from the beginning."

"How about I just skip to the end." I tossed my backpack at the foot of my bed. "He asked me to go out and I said no."

"No? You know what," Tasha tapped her foot, "I should just mush you in the head. Why did you tell him no?"

"Look, I'm not here for all that. I'm just here to do my year and then I'ma jet. That's it."

"I can't deal with you right now. This is not jail! One minute you wanna chill, and wondering if he likes you or not. Now he asks you out and instead of you going you trippin' and actin' all strange!"

"I'm not actin' strange! And, anyway, I don't have to explain anything to you; this is my life!"

"Then you need to live it!" she screamed, storming out of my room and slamming the door. A few seconds later, she flung the door open and said, "For your information, pitiful Pattie, Li'l Herman got us all into the Dough E. Fresh concert!"

"He..." Before I could finish my sentence, Tasha had slammed the door once more.

22

Ah Ya Know What...

It was the night of the concert, and me, Ebony, Reesie, and Tasha were all in Tasha's room, gettin' our fly on.

We wore matching light blue jeans, white tee shirts with our names airbrushed in bubble letters on them—courtesy of me, Vette-B—and crisp white, high-top Reeboks.

The only thing different was our hair. Reesie rocked a black lace bow tied around her ponytail. I wore my hair straight, spilling over my shoulders, with a stretchy sparkling gold headband. Ebony rocked her braids, and Tasha's hair was hooked up with crimps in the front and cascading coils in the back.

"This is my jam!" Tasha said as Dough E. Fresh's hit, *The Show,* blasted through the radio.

Reesie, at the mirror and applying hot pink eye shadow, free-styled: "We're just some fly chicks, that's gettin' right for the night. 'Cause when Dough E. Fresh rock up on the mic, he gon' rock the mic right!"

We all stopped what we were doin' and did the whop dance in agreement.

"Yo," I said, now helpin' Ebony lay her baby hair down. "What if Dough E. Fresh calls me up on stage?" I twirled around.

"He will call you," Reesie said, "right after he calls me."

"Y'all know he could call any of us," Tasha said.

"That would be stupid ill!" Reesie screamed, then popped her glossy lips.

"We should make a pact," Tasha said, "that if any of us get wit' Dough E. Fresh tonight, we hook everybody else up with one of his friends."

"What if some of his friends are broke?" Reesie curled her upper lip. "We don't know if all of his friends are rappers. Some of 'em might be project kings. And I already have one of those."

"Who?" I asked.

"My baby, Jerelle. That's who," Reesie said.

"You're still talking to Jerelle?" Ebony frowned. "I thought his phone was disconnected."

"I told you that in confidence! Not for you to diss my man and put him on Front Street. And for your information, it's back on now, thank you."

"Can we get back to Dough E. Fresh's friends?" Tasha said, "'Cause I don't wanna hear y'all arguing about Mr. Telephone Man, Jerelle. Now, let's scratch Dough E.'s friends and change it to rappers. So, if any of us get hooked up with Dough E., we have to hook the crew up with another rapper. I got Hammer."

"Eww," I said. "No way. 'Cause I got Rakim, baby! Yes! What! *Umm-hmm*! I ain't no joke."

"And I got Slick Rick," Reesie said in a bouncy British accent. "Just call me Sally."

We all cracked up.

"Since you all are all choosing someone else, then I might as well claim Dough E. Fresh," Ebony said.

"Don't even try it; we all have a chance at Dough E.," I said to Ebony.

"Yo," Tasha said, "we better take one last look in the mirror. Li'l Herman just beeped me 0377; that's code for he's on his way to get us."

We rushed over to the mirror, pressed shoulder to shoulder, and after we reassured one another that we were cute, I looked at each of their reflections and said, "I wanna tell y'all somethin'. But I don't want y'all buggin' or sayin' any slick comments."

"I wouldn't never do that," Reesie said. "And I can't stand chicks who act like that. Always running their mouths with some foolishness."

"Let's bow our heads. And have a moment of silence," Ebony said.

"Why?" we asked.

"Reesie is about to be struck by lightning. She's the main one who always has something slick to say, and suddenly, she can't stand chicks who act that way. Girl, please."

Reesie responded, "Ebony, green is so not your color. You need to stick with black."

"Would you two shut up and let Yvette speak. Dang!" Tasha said. "Go 'head, Yvette. Even if they're not listening, I am."

"I'm listening," Ebony said.

"Me too," Reesie agreed.

I took in their reflections again. I knew I was taking a

chance, but I had to tell somebody, or in this case, three somebodies. "IwannaletBrooklynknowthatI'mfeelin'him," I said in one breath.

They each paused, like they had to figure out what I'd just said; then their light bulbs went off and they screamed.

"Yes!" Tasha said. "Thank you, baby Jesus. 'Cause this heifer is a hard nut to crack."

"A nut?" Reesie looked concerned. "Wait a minute, Yvette. What does Tasha mean? Don't tell you're a herma-dyke."

"A what?" I frowned.

"A herma-dyke. It means you're swingin' with a litter box and a pipe."

"Oh, my God!" Ebony said.

Tasha blinked, like she couldn't believe this was happening. "First of all, it's *hermaphrodite*. And hard nut to crack is an expression."

Reesie put in her two cents worth. "Don't do that. Don't try and play me out and act like I'm crazy. 'Cause y'all would've been thinking the same thing. Anyway, Yvette, as you were *saying* before Tasha started calling you names..."

"I was just sayin' I like Brooklyn, and I would like to go out with him."

"Brooklyn?" Reesie said, surprised.

"Why did you say it like that?" I asked.

Reesie continued. "Just be careful 'cause Alesha told me that they was working on their relationship."

I rolled my eyes and sucked my teeth. "Alesha is a liar. She came at me the other day all crazy, 'cause Brooklyn was taking me home, and he checked her. Told her they were done, been done, and he was tired of her. So she needs to stop lyin'."

"Well, dang. Okay." Reesie smirked. "Next."

"Yeah, next," I snapped.

"Don't get mad at me," Reesie said. "And, anyway, I thought you'd brother-zoned him."

Tasha's eyes popped open in surprise.

These birds talk too much!

"Where you get that from?" I asked, peering at my big-mouth housemate, Tasha. "I never said that."

Reesie carried on. "Well, if it's a lie, blame Tasha. 'Cause she told Ebony, and Ebony told me, that Brooklyn asked you to go out and you told him no."

Ebony huffed. "I also told you that you talk too much, but I don't see you running to tell that."

Tasha looked at me. "I never said you brother-zoned him. I just said you turned his date down."

"Same thing," Reesie said.

"No, I *did not* brother-zone him," I said.

"So why did you turn his date down?" Ebony asked.

"I was just confused."

Tasha asked, "When are you going to tell him you want to go out with him?"

I shrugged. "I don't know."

"I know," Tasha said. "Tonight. Li'l Herman said that after the concert, his cousin is having an after-party. And I'm sure Brooklyn will be there."

"You think?" I asked.

Tasha said, "Yes, girl, you know Brooklyn and Li'l Herman got a serious bromance going on. They ain't going nowhere without the other being there."

"All right." I smiled. "Then tonight. It's goin' down!"

23

Ain't No Half-Steppin'

You know what/peep this

For the first time in my life, the here-and-now was all that mattered.

The live music.

The dope way Dough E. Fresh and Slick Rick stepped onto stage and rocked the crowd.

I was captivated.

Fascinated.

Feelin'...sixteen.

Runnin' wit' a crew that wasn't headed for a scheme or tryna create one.

Just partying to be partying.

Chillin' to be chillin'.

Finally, someplace beyond the block.

Don't cry/Dry your eyes!

At least two hundred people were shoulder to shoulder, rockin' to the beat and screamin' at the stage.

I leaned over to Tasha, who was throwin' her arms in the air and yelled, "I guess Li'l Herman got the juice!"

She snapped her fingers. "Yeah, girl. It seems so. And when he pulled up in that olive green '77 Cadillac Coupe Deville, I was like, wait a minute, now. Hold up, pimp." She grinned, like it was only a matter of time before Li'l Herman was the boo assigned to the weekend.

I twisted my lips and said, "That car was loud as hell and you know it. Even Ms. Glo was like, 'In a minute, that car gon' have me fightin' dead bodies.' "

"It wasn't that loud," Tasha said. "Aunty Glo always exaggerating. She ain't say all that when his daddy Big Herman was creepin' to the house, driving that same Cadillac."

I laughed. "Now you know you wrong. You ain't have to call Ms. Glo out like that."

"Tasha," Reesie leaned over and asked, "what was with all that foam and cushion falling from Li'l Herman's car's ceiling? I felt like it was snowing on me."

"Me too!" Ebony agreed. "And why is he rockin' a three-piece suit?"

" 'Cause his name needs to be Whack-Skee," I said.

Tasha frowned and shot us all a look. "Y'all are three of the most ungrateful tricks I've ever seen. Ya behinds could've walked. And Whack-Skee?" She rolled her eyes at me. "Slow down, Vette-B, 'cause you could be home watching repeats of *Good Times* on TV, or smelling the Bengay Aunty Glo rubs into her knees. But you're not. Why? 'Cause *Whack-Skee* got you in the place to be. You better check yo'self for you wreck yo'self."

Tasha glared at Reesie. "And you raggin' on his ride, Cheresse? At least he got one! What party-line Jerelle got? A disconnected line. And you, Ebony. For your information, Mother Earth, in order for him to get the car on a school night, so he could bring y'all unappreciative behinds to this sold-out concert, he lied and told his mama he was goin' to church!"

"Church?" Reesie asked. "It ain't even Sunday."

"And if he told her he was goin' to church," I said, "then why is he gettin' on stage 'bout to toss it up?"

E'rybody's eyes shifted to the stage, where Dough E. Fresh's hype crew brought people up and passed the mic around. Of course they skipped right over us, killin' our dreams of having a rapper in our life.

But whatever.

Li'l Herman was on stage and he looked like a straight clown—dressed in a metallic gold and black pin-stripe suit with shoulder pads, a tight vest, and black MC Hammer pants. "Is he throwin' up gang signs?" I asked, but nobody answered.

Li'l Herman rapped, "Ah one-two, ah one-two. My name is Li'l Herman and most wonder why, but it ain't 'cause in my pants is a little guy. I'm super fresh, yes I'm the best, and on my chest don't have to be an S. Ah one-two, ah one-two."

"That's my baby!" Tasha yelled. "Get 'em, baby! Show 'em what time it is!"

Me, Ebony, and Reese looked at each other. Our eyes said the same thing: Tasha was out of control.

Li'l Herman ended his rap and Tasha looked at us and said, "Now y'all know that was fresh."

Ebony and Reesie didn't say a word, but I had to live with this chick. "Yes!" I clapped. "Stupid-dumb-triple-fat-dope! He is straight spittin' bars!"

"You better recognize." Tasha grinned, as Li'l Herman

walked over and pulled her into his embrace. And for the rest of the concert they were hugged up. Tasha had her back pressed to Li'l Herman's chest, and his arms draped over her shoulders.

As the concert went on, Dough E. Fresh killed it. I'd never seen so many stars in one place. Slick Rick, Run–D.M.C., Kurtis Blow, MC Lyte, and Kool Moe Dee. By the time the concert was over, e'rybody was hyped.

"Yo, that was so dope!" I squealed.

"Thank you, Li'l Herman," we all said.

"You the man, baby!" Tasha hollered, holdin' Li'l Herman by the waist.

He popped his collar and said, "You know the night doesn't have to end. Remember I told you my cousin, Lottie, is having an after-party at his crib. He said we can come through. Unless y'all gotta go home and get ready for school."

Was Mr. Three-Piece-Suit, Mr. Lied-to-Get-the-Car, Mr. Booty-Ass Rhymin', Mr. Whack-Skee tryna be funny? School? Really? It was only ten o'clock. We had at least another hour or two before we had to be worried about gettin' ready for school. See, this is why I'm anti-sucker.

Li'l Herman continued. "It's up to you; y'all can roll if you want to, or I can take y'all home."

"We rollin'," Tasha said. "Ain't nobody worried about school."

24

Ah One-Two, One-Two

"Hurry up and tell me if my breath stinks." Reesie blew a puff of air in Ebony's face, causing Ebony to stagger back.

"What the hell?" Ebony blinked. "What have you been eating? I think I've been violated."

"Would y'all chill?" Tasha snapped. "I don't want them to think we're kids."

"Don't play me," Reesie said. "I'm no kid; and all I wanted to know was how my breath smelled. As matter of fact, Mrs. Li'l Herman, you need a Tic-Tac. *Mmph*. Unlike you, I don't wanna be in my future husband's face with my mouth smelling like unwashed feet."

"You mean ass." Ebony frowned, handing Reesie a pack of Red Hot gum. "Chew on all of that, at once."

"Whatever," Reesie said, poppin' a single stick of gum in her mouth.

"Tasha," Ebony called, "where did Li'l Herman go? How

he gon' invite us to an after party, then leave us sittin' in the car?"

"Word," Reesie agreed. "I'm tired of sittin' on this middle hump, holdin' this ceiling up."

"See, this is why I don't like to bring y'all nowhere. For your information, his cousin just moved out here to Virginia Beach, so Li'l Herman wanted to be sure this was the right house before we all walked up in there."

Reesie cut in, "Wait a minute, the right house? You can't be serious. I know he had to hear all that music playin' when he pulled up here. And I know he had to see all those people standing around kicking it. Either Li'l Herman lied and this ain't his cousin, or he up in there tellin' people he's our pimp. He ain't slick."

"*Shhh*, here they come," I said, and we all fell silent and looked straight ahead.

Li'l Herman walked over to the car and peeked in through the passenger side window. "This is my cuzo, Lottie," he said, pointing to the dude standing next to him.

All three of us in the back seat leaned forward.

"Dang, Daddy," Reesie mumbled. "You are deliciously cute."

"Yes. He. Is." Ebony whispered, "Reesie, gimme a piece of my gum back."

"Nope. Lottie"—Reesie boldly reached her hand across me and out the window—"I'm Cheresse, but everybody calls me Reesie. And I'm single." She pointed to me and Ebony. "These are my girls, Yvette and Ebony; they both tied up."

This chick is trippin'.

She carried on. "And Tasha is here with your cousin, Li'l Herman."

Lottie, who was the color of dark chocolate, smiled and a single dimple sank into his left cheek.

"Damn," Reesie said, droolin'. "Look at those teeth. They all straight too. No crowded mouth in sight. I mean that bottom left one is a li'l crooked, but, hey, ain't nobody perfect, except Jesus, and even Jesus had hard times."

Silence. Complete and utter silence.

Then Lottie said, "Are you all coming inside? I hope so, 'cause the house is all the way live."

"Oh, yes it is," Reesie replied, excited.

Li'l Herman opened the car door and helped Tasha out. Tasha then flipped up the front seat and we all climbed out the back.

"Lottie, this is my lady, Tasha." Li'l Herman grinned.

His lady?

Lottie looked over at me and Ebony. "I know she said your names were Yvette and Ebony, but I'm not sure who's who."

"I'm Ebony." She waved.

"And I'm Yvette," I said.

Lottie smiled. "Okay. Wassup, Ebony?" Before she could answer, Lottie continued. "Yvette, nice to meet you." His eyes soaked in e'ry part of me, causing me to wonder if I needed some gum. How was my hair? Was it all in place? Was my outfit still on point, or lookin' crazy?

"You look beautiful," Lottie said. "Maybe..."

"Lottie!" A car parked in front of Li'l Herman's car, and a guy stuck his head out the window. "Wassup?!"

"Yo! Yo!" Lottie yelled over to him, then looked back to us. "Check it; y'all go on in the house and make your-selves comfortable. I'll be in there in a minute. The music is bumpin', drinks flowin', and tons of food." He tossed me a soft wink, as he took a few steps backwards before turning around and walking over to the dudes who'd just called for his attention.

Reesie grinned. "Y'all know Lottie checkin' for me, right? Did you see how he was just lookin' at me? He was all in my grill."

Nobody even responded to that. Instead, we walked up the driveway and into the small brick house, where a live DJ rocked the mic, the music was jumpin' and people were e'rywhere. Some dancin', some drinkin', and some just kickin' it.

"My man, Fifty Grand! Li'l Herman!" came from behind us.

Brooklyn.

I didn't turn around. There was no way I could. I wasn't ready to face him yet.

I needed a mirror and a moment to get myself together.

Quickly, I walked away from my crew in search of the bathroom. After making a quick right down the hall, I found it, rushed in, and fell against the back of the door.

Breathe.

Breathe.

Chill.

You gon' really need to get yourself together. You cannot stop breathin' e'rytime Brooklyn walks into the room. One day you gon' pass out. Plus, he ain't even all that.

Lies.

I looked at myself in the mirror, brushed a few strands of flying stray hair out of my face and tucked it back in its place. Refreshed my lip gloss. Then said to myself, "Just go out there, act like you have some sense, and say, 'Brooklyn, does that date still stand?'"

No, that sounds stupid.

I got it. Say, "You wanna hang out?"

Ugh. That sounds even dumber.

"Just say..."

Someone pounded on the door.

"I'm coming," I said. I shook my head and took one last peek in the mirror. "I don't know what I'm going to say, but I'ma say something."

I opened the door and some eye-rollin' heifer stood there. Whatever. I ignored her, kept walkin' and slam!

God must hate me.

I'd marched right into Brooklyn, practically knocked out his heartbeat.

He looked down. "Bricks?" He paused and my eyes drew in his fly red Adidas sweat suit, gold dookey rope chain, and Stan Smith Adidas sneakers. He continued. "Hey, I thought that was you out there, but you walked away so fast, I wasn't sure."

"Oh, for real?" I wondered if I sounded as crazy as I felt. "I didn't even see you. So, *umm*, what are you doin' here? Were you at the concert?"

"Fa'sho' I was at the concert. Li'l Herman told me he got y'all in. I was hoping we would meet up and I'd get to see you. Especially since you're up in here, looking fine as wine."

Dear God. I loooooove his southern accent. I swear country boys are better than Ms. Glo's pancakes.

He tucked my hair behind my ear. "Lookin' all purty."

I sighed, seconds away from takin' my hands and making a heart symbol.

Okay, Jesus. Work with me. Please help me to sound

just as chill as he does. "Appreciate you peepin' that," I said.

Shoot me now. Why did I say that? Ugh! Just smile and figure out a way to say, "I wanna kick it sometime."

He laughed. "So thank you is not an option, huh?"

"Thank you for what?" I paused. "Oh, wait. No I didn't mean to say it like that. I meant thank you; you look nice too."

You are dying by the moment. Just tell him! Tell! Him!

"Brooklyn, I *umm* was wonderin' if, *umm*, we could—..."

"Oh, here you are," came from behind us.

I turned around.

It was some strange chick invading our moment.

I turned back to Brooklyn and said, "So I was thinkin' that we should..."

"Brooklyn, I was looking all over for you." The girl walked around and stood next to him.

Oh, hell no! I gave this tramp the gas face. "Is this how they do rudeness in the south?" I said to the girl. "I know you heard us having an A-B conversation. So you really need to see your way out of it. Unless of course, you two are booed up or somethin'?" I looked dead into Brooklyn's face and waited for an answer.

"I'm sorry," the girl said. "I'm Jacinda."

Oh, that would be a yes, they're together.

Jacinda continued. "I didn't catch your name."

And that would be a hell, yes.

She held out her hand.

Trick, you'll find a bridge and a strong wind before I'll ever shake your hand.

I left her hangin'.

"This is Bricks," Brooklyn said, his eyes bright, like he was seconds from smiling.

Bricks? Boy, don't you ever call me Bricks again!

"Yvette," I corrected him. "My name is Yvette."

"Oh, okay. That's sweet," Jacinda said sounding completely fake.

Man-eater, I wasn't talkin' to you!

Chill. Let it go and let her live.

I shot a glance over at the tramp. "Well, I'ma let y'all get back to ya li'l date." I turned around.

"Bricks," Brooklyn called, "wait!"

I wish the hell I would.

Seconds later, I stood in the middle of the crowded living room floor looking for a way to melt into the carpet. "Did you see Brooklyn?" Tasha asked, as she and Reesie rushed over to me.

"We just saw him!" Reesie said. "And he was here with some punk-rock, *Breakfast Club* lookin' ho. I was like, oh hellll nooooo, not today! I gotta find my girl. Now tell me do you wanna jump this trick, 'cause Tasha ain't gave a good bitch-slap in a minute."

Tasha blinked. "Why are you keeping track of my bitch slaps?"

Reesie carried on. "I'm just sayin'. Or, Yvette, we could get Ebony to go outside and slash Brooklyn's tires. 'Cause I know, for sure, she's got a box cutter in her purse. After all, she lives in the projects. Or you wanna just chill and move on? 'Cause truthfully, Brooklyn ain't worth the drama. And I don't think he's cute. I think he's okay. But you're my girl, so if you wanna roll, just let me know. 'Cause I'm the friend who's gon' stand back, watch y'all duke it out and make sure don't nobody else get in it."

"Negative to all of that," I said. "If I wanted to gun for that trick, I would've already taken her down and had her wonderin' what happened. But I'm not that interested." I looked over to Tasha. "We need to get ready to go."

"What?" She looked taken aback. "We just got here. I know you upset because of Brooklyn and all but don't put the brakes on me. Li'l Herman is about to be captain of my week."

"Did you forget that we have a curfew? I'm not tryna mess that up. You can make Li'l Herman captain tomorrow."

"Would you chill?" Tasha snapped.

"Both y'all got a point though," Reesie said. "'Cause y'all know Ms. Glo is crazy. She don't play that. But on the other hand, Yvette, you sound a li'l green right now. Just a li'l bit."

"Whatever. I'm just sayin' we need to roll," I answered.

"Stop being so uptight," Tasha insisted.

"I'm not bein' uptight. I just don't want any problems."

Tasha huffed. "Look, Aunty Glo will be sleeping when we get in anyway. She sleeps hard as hell, and she won't even know what time we get home."

I didn't say a word; I just shot her a look.

"Oh wait," Reesie said, "somebody pause the world, honey. I have spotted a cutie and he is looking this way. Yvette, you gon' have to take this one for the team."

Tasha whined, "Yvette, I promise we won't get into any trouble. I'm just tryna have a good time, and you should too. Lottie looked like he was interested in you; maybe you should see what's up with him."

"Lottie? I don't like him."

"Well, find you something to do like, 'cause I need to find Li'l Herman and get my dance on."

"Tasha, we need to be leavin' in an hour."

"Yeah, an hour," she agreed.

"I'm serious. One hour; then we need to jet."

"Bet," she said and took off, leaving me standing in the middle of the floor lookin' lost.

Two hours later

I needed a cigarette.

Newport.

Extra Menthol.

And a Forty.

Ole English.

Straight to the head.

Tasha was actin' shot out over Li'l Herman. The same dude who just the other day in class she didn't care if he was on fire; now he was lightin' her world.

Reesie was hugged up with some break dancer.

Ebony kicked it with an up-and-coming rapper named Black Conscious.

Brooklyn was slow draggin' with the ugly trick he brought to the party.

Me?

I just sat there. On the couch, next to some stutterin' sweat monster who had attempted to ask me to dance five times to four different songs, from Planet Rock to Cool G. Rap. Now EPMD's "You Gots to Chill" played and he was at it again.

"Caaaaaaa..."

Ugh!

"IIIIIIIIIIII..."

I couldn't stand it a moment longer. "You wanna dance?"

He smiled. "Yaaaaa."

"Come on."

I got up, determined to make the best out of this moment. I moved my shoulders and just as I picked up a sweet beat with my feet, whyyyyyy did this fool break out into a Michael Jackson kick and scream, "Ah hee-hee?!"

What the? I took a step back, 'cause in a minute his flyin' kick was gon' knock me in the face.

I was still tryna groove, though. Plus, my girls were all sayin', "Go 'head, Yvette! Work it out!" So I was tryna show 'em a li'l Jersey style.

Failed.

'Cause this fool started backin' it up and doin' Da Butt.

And what did I do? Left him standin' right there while I walked back over to the dead corner of the room and took a seat on the plastic-covered red velour couch.

"That your dude?" Brooklyn asked, walking over to me.

"Is that your girl?" I snapped.

"My girl?" he asked, taken aback.

"Don't act surprised. Y'all was extra cuddled up over by the bathroom. And all that bumpin' and grindin' you two did across the floor was ridiculous."

"We weren't cuddled up, and we weren't bumpin' and grindin' across the dance floor. Anyway, why would you care so much?"

"I don't. I'm just sayin' maybe you two need a short stay. Go get you a motel room or somethin'; just get outta my face with it."

He laughed. "Bricks, you buggin'. I asked you out. You turned me down and when I asked you why, you told me

'Cause.' So I figured if *cause* was a good enough reason for you not to go out with me, then it was a good enough reason for me not to sweat you about it."

"I didn't ask you to sweat me!"

"Anybody ever tell you that you're cute when you get mad?" he said.

"Anybody ever tell you that homegirl is across the room, lookin' for you, again."

He turned around, and as he held up his index finger for her to give him a moment, I walked away.

Another hour passed. The party was still goin' strong, and Tasha begged for fifteen more minutes.

I was fallin' asleep and was slowly dissolving into this couch's plastic cover. I lifted one thigh to get it unstuck, and I swore it sounded just like a record had screeched. Lifted the other thigh; now two records screeched. "What's wrong, my party's boring you?"

Lottie.

"At this moment, it's not the party. It's your couch. It's eating me," I said.

He laughed. "Come over here and let's sit at the bar." He pointed into the dining room, where he had a full-service glass bar. "You might be a little more comfortable over there."

I agreed.

"So, what are you drinking?" Lottie asked, as I hopped up on the barstool.

"Nothin'. I'm cool," I said.

"You have to let me get you a drink. It's the least I can do. I've been around here all night, making connections for my music, and all I really wanted to do was get at you. So tell me, what you want, a glass of wine?"

"I'm cool, seriously. Plus, I'm only in high school," I said, strugglin' to sound innocent, like I'd never had a drink before.

"How old are you?" he asked.

"Sixteen."

"As pretty as you are, I thought you were at least twenty."

I laughed. "Yeah, right. How old are you?" I asked. He didn't look a day over seventeen. And with the exception of the seven inches of hair stacked on top of his fade, he wasn't that much taller than me and he was boney.

He said, "I'm twenty-five."

Twenty-five? I'm so tired of these old men. Where is Tasha?

"Are you sure you don't want anything to drink?" he asked. "Let me get you a soda or something."

"Really, it's okay."

"You're breaking my heart."

"I don't mean to. I'm just tired. And ready for my friend, Tasha, to come on so we can go."

Lottie looked at his watch. "Already? It's just a few minutes after midnight."

"But I need to get home."

"Y'all look cute," Tasha said, walking over and pressing her shoulder into mine.

"We need to get ready to go," I said.

"Yeah," she agreed. "In a minute." She started to dance. "Come on Li'l Herman; this is my jam!"

Lottie smiled and I sighed.

"Well," Lottie said, "I guess at least I'll get another minute."

"Yeah, seems so," I answered.

"So, you go to school with my cousin?" he asked.

"Yeah. Me and my daughter just moved here not too long ago."

"Oh, you have a daughter?" He looked shocked. "Word?"

"Yeah."

"How old?" he asked.

"Two."

He paused. "How old are you again?"

"Sixteen."

"Wow, you had her at fourteen."

I nodded.

"Still with her father?"

"No." I think I said that a little too fast.

"And from the way you said that, I guess you ain't never goin' back."

"Never." I smiled. "So what about you? Since you all up in my B.I., what's up with you? You got a girlfriend?"

"Nah. I'm single."

"Ai'ight," I said, as Luther Vandross's "If This World Were Mine" played. "I love this song!" I swayed in my seat.

"Well, I guess this dance is on me." Lottie took my hand and we danced until we couldn't dance anymore. Then we laughed, joked, and chilled, until the night rolled into the morning, and the sun made its way into the sky.

25

Five...Four...Three... Two...One...

Time's up.

I walked into Ms. Glo's living room and saw Janette, my social worker, sittin' on the couch, waitin' for me.

The look on Ms. Glo's face was more than pissed; it was disappointed. Disappointed that I'd came in here a screw-up, and a month later, was gon' leave out one.

Ms. Glo looked at Tasha. "Go to your room." She turned to me. "Yvette, you stay right there."

"Aunty Glo," Tasha said, her eyes pleading for understanding.

"Did you hear what I said?" Ms. Glo said sternly.

"Yes, ma'am, but..."

"I said go."

Tasha tossed me a pitiful eye, then dragged to her room.

This was it.

I would never be more than I was at this moment.

I should beg her to let me stay.

No.

Beggin' don't work. It never convinced Mommy to stay.

You going back to jail…

Officer Washington.

Kamari in foster care.

Nana.

Stick.

You ain't gon' never be shit.

Flip.

I got some rock to make you feel better.

Tears filled my eyes.

You better not cry.

You better not drop one tear.

I couldn't help it and before I could save my pride from the embarrassment of desperation I said, "I'm sorry, Ms. Glo. I didn't mean to stay out all night."

"Be quiet," Ms. Glo said.

I couldn't be quiet. I had to explain. "We were at the concert, but the promoter had an after-party. And we were only supposed to be there for a while. But one thing led to another, and another thing led to this morning and…"

Janette jumped up. "Yvette! What were you doing staying out all night? Were you drinking? Doing drugs?"

"It's my fault!" Tasha rushed into the living room. "I was the one who said we should stay. Yvette wanted to go. And no she wasn't high or drunk; it wasn't that kind of party."

"Young lady," Janette said, "I'm speaking to Yvette." She looked at me. "Yvette?"

"No, I wasn't doing any of that!" I said.

Janette tapped her foot and shook her head in disgust. "This is it. You have to go. You cannot stay here. This is a violation. Flat-out against the rules." She looked at Ms.

Glo. "You told me you sent her to the store early this morning. Why did you tell me that?"

"Because I knew what would happen if I didn't tell you something. So now you know the truth. But I think you're overreacting."

"I'm not overreacting! Yvette, go pack yours and Kamari's things. I have to call the office. This isn't the right place for you two."

I didn't move.

"Look," Ms. Glo said to Janette. "When you all called me and asked me to take Yvette, I said yes, because I felt like I could help her. I never expected her to be perfect. And I didn't know you expected perfection either. Yeah, she screwed up. So what? You've never messed up before? Your visit was unexpected; otherwise, she would have been here."

"She should have been here whether she knew I was coming or not. She's a mother!" Janette looked at me. "And a mother doesn't abandon her child for a party!"

"Hold on here!" Ms. Glo was pissed. "She didn't abandon her child! I was here with Kamari; and furthermore, Yvette's a child. Did you forget that? Is there any room in your rulebook for her to be one? Now I know you have a job to do, but I'm asking you to leave her here with me, because if you take her and that baby out of here today, we will lose both of them to the streets. Is that what you want? Can you live with that?"

"This isn't about me." Janette paused, pursed her red lips, and soaked in a thought. "I want the best for Yvette too."

"The best is here with me," Ms. Glo insisted.

Janette paused again and once more stared off into a

thought, then cast a look my way. "Yvette, this can never happen again. Ever."

"It won't," I reassured her.

"It better not. Because you don't have another chance. This is it for you. There are a lot of kids who'd love to be in your shoes; don't mess it up." Janette gathered her tote bag and purse. "I have to get going for now, but I will be back."

"I understand," I said. "But I won't mess this up."

She responded with a smirk and a wave goodbye.

Ms. Glo walked her to the door, shook her hand, then watched Janette get into her car. Once she took off and rounded the corner, Ms. Glo whipped around to face me and Tasha and said, "Let me tell y'all behinds somethin'. As you can see, this is not a game and I ain't playin' with neither one of you. I'm not your sister or either one of y'all girlfriends. And I may not be your mother, but I am the mother of this house, and what I say absolutely goes."

"We were..." me and Tasha said simultaneously, both trying to explain.

"Be quiet!" she yelled. "Here I was worried about the two of you all night. I didn't know where you were. Didn't know who to call. Didn't even know where to start looking. Then you walk in here looking half crazy and smelling questionable. Were you two drinking? Were you getting high? And don't lie!"

"No," we swore.

"It was just a party," Tasha said. "A party."

"You two have a curfew, yet neither one of y'all had any sense to be here on time. You weren't even an hour late. You stayed out all night! You're too young to be in a bar, and teen night at the club ends at twelve. So where were you, 'cause the only thing open all night are legs."

Tasha said, "Ms. Glo, we were at a house party; that's it. We didn't drink; we didn't smoke. We didn't get high. Wasn't no sleeping around. We danced, laughed, and chilled...it just went on too long. Yvette was the one who kept saying let's go. It was me who wanted to stay."

"So you chose not to do the right thing," Ms. Glo said. "That's what you're telling me. You knew you were wrong, but you gon' do what you wanna do, anyway."

"No," I said.

"Looks that way to me," Ms. Glo insisted.

"That's not what I meant," Tasha said.

Ms. Glo continued. "You girls have the chance to be anything you wanna be. And, Yvette, you have Kamari, so if you blow it for you, you're blowing it for the two of you. Don't let that happen."

"I won't," I promised Ms. Glo. "And I'm really sorry."

"Me too," Tasha said.

"Stop being sorry and start being sincere," Ms. Glo snapped. "Now enough standing around; you two need to go and get ready for school."

"School?" me and Tasha both said, surprised. "We haven't had any sleep."

"Whose problem is that? Not mine. It's a school day, and like my mama used to say, 'If you go out with the girls at night, then you need to be up with the women in the morning.' Well, good morning."

26

Push It...

"Good morning, Yvette," Mrs. Brown, the school guidance counselor, said, a little too chipper, like we'd bumped into each other at Dairy Queen. When the truth was, a few minutes after Janette left the house that morning, Mrs. Brown called and said she needed to see me before homeroom, makin' it obvious that Janette had requested a "Save Yvette" intervention.

Whatever. I showed up. Now I was here, sitting in the chair next to Mrs. Brown's desk, praying she would cut through the crap and just say what she had to say.

"So how are things going?" she asked, pulling her square reading glasses down the bridge of her nose and placing them on her desk. She picked up a paper clip and flipped it between her thumb and index finger.

"Mrs. Brown, no disrespect, but my patience is short. And I've been in the system long enough to know that my caseworker called you. So can we just get to the point? 'Cause I really wanna go to homeroom."

She stopped flipping the paperclip. "Okay." She nodded. "Yes, Janette called me this morning, really upset, saying you'd stayed out all night partying and doing God knows what."

I rolled my eyes. "God knows what? So you're another one who thinks I was out gettin' high, drinkin', and havin' sex?"

"Were you?" she asked.

"Hell, yes!" I snapped my fingers. "Of course I was. First I smoked crack; afterwards, I snorted a line of dope. Chased it with a Forty. That got me zooted enough to participate in the orgy. And before the night was over, I slashed a few faces for sport."

Mrs. Brown sighed. "Don't be a smart aleck, Yvette. Your caseworker knows the consequences of you breaking the rules and not doing well here."

"And what, you don't think I know what the consequences are?"

"I certainly hope you do. And I also hope you know that Ms. Glo was the only home that would take you."

"I *know that* too," I snapped.

"Janette's worried. We're all worried. And I wish you would see that."

I huffed. "You know what I wish? I wish y'all would stop sweatin' me and get off my back. I wish I could screw up wit' out e'rybody havin' a panic attack. Or sayin' I did this or that. Yes, I stayed out too late. Not because I was gettin' high, drinkin' or doin' anything crazy. I went to a concert, then an after-party. We danced, we laughed, we kicked it... like I have never kicked it before. The only crime I committed was goin' to a party and stayin' too long."

"Why didn't you call home and tell Ms. Glo?"

"Because it didn't cross my mind," I said.

"You know she had to be worried about you."

"She told me that. I apologized. It will not happen again. Okay? Can I go now?"

"No. We're not done. I want you to tell me why you're so uptight and agitated this morning?"

I leaned forward in my chair, 'cause this trick was buggin'. "Mrs. Brown, can you imagine livin' somewhere—that's not your home—but is your home, 'cause you ain't got no other home. You don't have no family. Nobody. And you live with people who the state assigns to you as your family. You get comfortable with them, you almost love them, and then one day your caseworker shows up and says, 'You have to come with me.' You don't know where you're goin'. Hell, she don't even know where you're goin', but you goin'.

"Can you imagine livin' a life like that? Being on edge like that, e'ryday, all day? Meanwhile, e'rybody's tellin' you to live and enjoy the moment. But when you do step out and live—just a li'l bit—enjoy the moment and party a few hours too long, e'rybody wonderin' if you're high, drunk, or somewhere sexin' your problems away?"

I paused and let her absorb what I'd said. Then I continued. "Nobody ever sees how you're strugglin' to un-learn e'rything you know. You can't cuss no more. You gotta watch your temper. You gotta go to school. You gotta learn how to be cute, how to properly giggle, how to sit still, how to be a child, when you was born grown.

"All this new shit, e'rybody expects you to know, but nobody ever stopped to teach you. You're just expected to figure it out. And if you screw up and don't live up to e'rybody else's expectations, then you must be retarded, stupid, ungrateful, or blind not to see that e'rybody's worried."

"Yvette," Mrs. Brown said, "you don't need to carry all of that weight around."

"Listen, what I need is a freakin' break. I just want to live, for once. And if I mess up, I don't need the world to stop spinnin'."

She stared at me. "Yvette, I just want what's best for you."

If I hear that one more time, I'ma scream.

"They must be runnin' a special on that line today," I said, exhausted. "You want that. Janette wants that. Ms. Glo wants that. And believe it or not, even Yvette wants that."

"You're doing well. The teachers all say you're a pleasure to have in class. You're doing great with your schoolwork. And I don't want to see anything get in the way of that. Especially not a party."

"The only thing that can get in the way of me not doin' the right thing is me."

She smiled and nodded in agreement.

"Now. Mrs. Brown. Can I *please* leave?"

She glanced up at the clock. "Yeah. You can go."

"So, what did she say?" Tasha grabbed my hand the moment I stepped out of Mrs. Brown's office and pulled me into the girls' bathroom. "Was she pissed off? Buggin' out? I was tryna listen through the door, but I couldn't hear nothin'."

Tasha checked each bathroom stall to be sure they were empty. "Okay, it's just us in here." She leaned against the pink tiled wall, across from the full mirror. "Tell me. What'd she say? Your caseworker really called her?"

"Yeah, she called her." I sat down on the counter, next to the sink. "Mrs. Brown was cool, for the most part. She just pissed me off asking me why I was mad. I'm like, for real, yo—first of all, I haven't had any sleep."

"Word," Tasha said. "We can't party like that again. Not on a school night."

"We can't party like that, period," I said. "We have a curfew. And as you can see, not being home by the time we were supposed to be almost went completely left for me."

"I know. And I feel real bad about that." Tears filled her eyes.

I continued. "I know you didn't mean any harm, but I need you to hear me on this: When I say it's time to leave, that it's gettin' close to curfew, we gotta go. I don't need anybody lookin' for me. Unlike you, I'm here on a plea bargain. I need to chill for a year. I don't wanna go back to jail. I don't want my baby in foster care. My caseworker is not playin' with me."

"I'm sorry," Tasha said. "I feel horrible about how everything went down. If you and Kamari had to leave because of me"—tears wet her cheeks—"I don't know what I would ever do. I don't really have a family either, Yvette. And you and Kamari, and Aunty Glo, y'all are like my family. If this means we gotta stay in the house all day, every day, and not ever hang out again, I'm willing to do that. I'm willing to make sure you have a great and drama-free year. I can promise you that. I will be on my best behavior. No more shenanigans."

My chuckle started out as a disbelieving snicker, then

turned into a full on hardy laugh. "Heifer, shut up. This is not the *Young and the Restless*. You know how you sound? The only thing missin' was some theme music. Nobody said we couldn't hang out. I'm not about to sit in the house all day, every day. We just can't hang out all night. Period. And you and Ms. Glo...y'all kind of feel like family to me too."

"Awww, we do?" Tasha walked over and snatched me into a hug. "I finally got a baby sister."

"What are y'all in here goin' through?" The bathroom door flew open and Reesie walked in. "Wait, wait, wait. Please don't tell me that after stayin' out all night, y'all got the black knocked off you too?" She wrapped her arms around us and joined in on the hug. "Yo, don't feel bad, 'cause my mother, Barbara, she wasn't playin'. She was like, don't you ever stay out all night! And Ebony, I couldn't even get her on the phone this morning. I think she's Ivory now."

The bell rang.

"Come on," Reesie said. "Let's get it together. Cheer up. Tasha, you were pale yellow anyway, so in a couple of hours you'll be back in full force. And, Yvette, well, once you spend some time in the sun, your color will come back. I promise. Now let's go; we gotta get to homeroom."

"Yo, so did y'all bone after you took her home?" was the loud whisper that came from the back of class, as me, Reesie, and Tasha took our seats in homeroom. Most of the kids were still coming into the classroom, while Mr. Harris threatened those who lingered in the hallway with Saturday detention.

The loud whisper continued. "'Cause if not, I want my five dollars."

"Who said that?" Tasha whispered to me and Reesie.

"Well, the only ones who sit back there are Brooklyn, Li'l Herman, James, and Rasheed," I said.

"I wonder who they're talkin' about," Tasha mused.

Reesie murmured, "It sounds like they're talkin' about a stank ho skeezer."

"Shh," I said. "Don't be so loud; just listen."

"That wasn't the bet," the loud whisper said.

"That was Li'l Herman," Tasha said. "I know his voice. And what bet?"

Li'l Herman continued. "The bet was that if we got busy, y'all were supposed to give me five dollars."

Tasha's eyes popped open wide. "Get busy? Wit' who?" she whispered, pissed.

"You the stank ho skeezer, Tasha?" Reesie asked. "You let him bust out the Jimmy on the first night?"

"Heck no!" Tasha said.

Reesie said, "Then what bet is he talking about? Oh, my God, don't tell me he's cheating on you already? Good thing you didn't clear your week."

"Quiet," Mr. Harris said as he took out his roll-book.

"Yo, Herman," James said, "that was not the bet. The bet was that if you hit it last night, we'd pay you five dollars. Otherwise, you had to pay us."

"Nah," Li'l Herman carried on, struggling to whisper, "you got it wrong. 'Cause I would've never made a bet like that. Me and Tasha just started kicking it."

"Tasha, yes, *you are* the stank ho skeezer," Reesie whispered. "And Li'l Herman placed a bet on your coochie. A cheap one, too. You couldn't at least get ten dollars? He needs to be cussed out for that. Don't tell me you gon' let him play you out like that!"

Li'l Herman continued. "She ain't that easy. I need more than a day. I need at least two days. We're supposed to hang out after school today. So this time tomorrow I'ma be pimp-walkin' in here and y'all gon' be like, 'What's that smell?' And I'ma be like, 'Cherries, dawg. Cherries.'"

Tasha stood up and turned around to face Li'l Herman. She shoved both hands up on her hips and swung her neck in full motion. "Have you lost yo' rabbit-behind mind?!"

Immediately the class became silent. A few seconds later, e'rybody burst into oohs, ahhs, and giggles as Tasha continued. "Boy, you will never get this. So you might as well pay 'em all of your li'l allowance money, 'cause I'm done with you. And the only cherries they gon' smell will be from the hand lotion you use, jerk-off!"

"What is goin' on in here?!" Mr. Harris demanded to know.

"Chill, Tasha," Li'l Herman said. "I wasn't talkin' about you."

"Lies! I heard you!"

"Break it up! Break it up!" Mr. Harris marched over to Tasha and Li'l Herman. "Last I checked, I didn't have Ike and Tina in my class! Now you two either cut it out or you will be sent to the office for..."

Brgggggg!

The bell rang. We all popped out of our seats, and Mr. Harris's threat was lost in the shuffle of our feet.

"Bricks!" Brooklyn called me as I walked past him and hurried down the hall. "Can't speak?"

I turned to face him but never stopped walking. "Yes. I can speak. But I'm not." I rushed over to my locker and grabbed the books for my next two classes. I turned around and Brooklyn was standing there.

"Why are you always in my way?" I asked, not knowing what else to say.

"I'm tryin' to be in your way."

"And why is that?"

"I wanna know why you're trippin'."

"Psst. Please," I said, more to myself than to him. Besides, I ain't owe him no explanation as to whether I was trippin' or not.

And for the record, I wasn't trippin'.

I had tripped, and that's why I ignored him, or was at least tryin' to. Especially since I'd seen him last night, all cuddled up on his whack-behind date. I couldn't stop thinkin' about how I should've been the trophy on his arm.

"Excuse you, stalker," I said as I tapped Brooklyn on his shoulder, "but I need to get to my next class."

"Are all up-north girls like this?" he asked.

I frowned. 'Cause I know he ain't want me to get started on down-south country boys. "And what's that supposed to mean? Like what?"

"One day you're cool and the next day you're buggin'."

I curled my upper lip, hopin' to put a stop to this dumb smile I felt creepin' up. Brooklyn was so stupid fresh. He rocked a pair of razor-creased red Levi jeans, with a matching Levi jacket, a white tee, with two gold dookey rope chains hanging around his neck, and on his feet were Air Jordans.

I sucked my teeth and shot him a look. "Boy. Please. Spare. Me."

He continued. "At least tell me what the problem is. 'Cause after today, I'm not gon' ask again."

Oh no he didn't! "I didn't *ask you* to *ask me* the first time. So don't act like I'm sweatin' you."

"I didn't say you were sweatin' me. All I asked was what did I do to you? Clearly, I'm checkin' for you. I asked you on a date and you told me 'cause. Which I guess in Jersey means no. But down here means nothing, because 'cause is not even a complete thought. Which means that your 'cause ain't nothing more than you fronting. So I'm stepping to you, like a man, and I'm asking you what's the deally-o, yo? If you don't like me, cool. We can be friends. But this never-ending attitude with me gotta stop. Today."

Is that an order? Okay. He comin' at me all strong and gangster-like. He just upped his cutie meter by at least a thousand. And if I don't like you? Boy, you are so fine, your name should be Mine.

I said, "You asked me out. Then because I didn't say yes, you gon' show up at a party, where you knew I'd be, with a date to throw in my face? How played is that? What did you expect me to do, run after you? You better fetch Alesha for that."

Brooklyn laughed, and oh I hated that I loved his laugh.

I continued, "Oh, you think this is funny? I'ma joke now?"

"No," he answered in a serious voice, takin' a step too close to me. "I don't think you're a joke. I think you're purty. And I think you like me, but for whatever hard-to-get reason you wanna push me away. And as far as ole girl. I met her at the party. And I left her there."

Now what are you gon' say to that? I don't know. Think. Think. Think. I can't. Wait, I got it. "Whatever."

"Yeah, you say 'whatever' when you know I'm tellin' the truth. Check it, Bricks."

"Yvette," I corrected him.

He stepped completely into my personal space, lightly placed his forehead against mine and whispered, "When you're ready for me, let me know. But see this li'l back and forth game, I'm not good wit' that." He boldly kissed me on my forehead, before walkin' away and leavin' me frozen in place.

27

Love Saw It

Just say, hey, Ms. Glo…
No.
Okay, okay. I got it. I'ma just be like, hey, Ms. Glo,
wassup?
No.
She is not my homie. Just say, hey, Ms. Glo, can I speak
to you for a minute? Yeah, that might work. Suppose she
says no? She ain't gon' say no.
I don't know that.
She's not.
Ugh!

My thoughts made me madder by the minute. Meanwhile, Tasha and Reesie ran their mouths all the way home, about where Ebony could be and why she didn't come to school today. I really wanted to tell them to shut up, but I ain't wanna seem insensitive.

"I'ma stop by there on my way home," Reesie said, as we stood on Ms. Glo's porch. "I want to be sure she's still breathing. 'Cause you know her mama is a li'l touched. And y'all don't know this, but Ebony's stepfather and her grandmother both died in the same year. And they all lived in the house together."

I blinked, confused. "That's sad and all, but what does them dying in the same year have to do with anything?"

Reesie said, "*The same year*? And they *all lived in the same house. Together*. Now Ebony has disappeared." She arched a brow. "Without a trace. What does that sound like to you?"

Tasha nodded. "You got a point, Reesie. All three of us should go over there and see what's up."

"Time out," I said, holding my hands up and placing my right palm over my left fingertips. "Time out. Y'all been watchin' too much TV. This is not *21 Jump Street*. And if you tryna say Ebony's mother took her out, then what is we goin' over there for? So we can be the next to go? I ain't tryin' to die. Nah. I ain't doin' that."

"She is not going to take us out," Reesie insisted.

"If she killed her own daughter, what do you think she gon' do to you? No thank you, ma'am. If you come back, I'll know how it worked out for you. But me? I'm goin' in the house, where it's safe, with Ms. Glo and my baby."

"Well, I'ma go," Tasha said. "I'm just not gon' go inside to see Ebony. She can come to the door."

"Bet. We'll walk around the back and knock on her bedroom window," Reesie said. "That way, if we hear or see anything suspicious, we can haul ass."

"Why can't you two just call her on the phone? Or better, wait and see if she comes to school?"

Reesie answered quickly. "That's too long. Plus, I need to know if she's dead before my brother, June Bug, makes his ABC store run. Just in case I need a small bottle of brown liquor to pour out."

"That's a good point," Tasha agreed.

"Okay. Well, y'all let me know, and I'll bring the teddy bear and the balloons. But until then, I'm tired and I'm goin' in the house." And I left both of their crazy behinds standin' there.

Just say...Ms. Glo...Ugh!

It wasn't that I didn't know what to say to Ms. Glo, I just didn't know how to say it.

I tossed my backpack on the floor in my room and kicked my sneakers off. Then I walked to Ms. Glo's bedroom and leaned against the door frame.

Ms. Glo leafed through a *Jet* magazine, as Kamari rolled around on the foot of Ms. Glo's bed, easy and free, full of giggles. Kamari rolled to the edge of the bed and just when it seemed she were about to fall, Ms. Glo kicked her leg out to stop Kamari from hittin' the floor. And Kamari would do it all over again.

"That looks like fun," I said.

"Mommy!" Kamari jumped off the bed and ran over to me, huggin' me around my legs. "I missed you."

"I missed you too," I said.

Kamari was bubbling over with excitement. "I got ice cream. Went on the swing. We sang One-Two-Three song."

"Wow! That sounds like an amazing day!" I looked over at Ms. Glo. "Hey, Ms. Glo, how was your day?"

"Restful." She smiled. "How was yours? You look sleepy."

"Funny," I chuckled, "I am sleepy. I haven't had any sleep today. Tasha will be right back. She just went with Reesie to Ebony's."

"Okay. You didn't want to go?"

"No." I shook my head. "I wanted to come inside and see Kamari. And talk to you."

"Talk to me about what?" She placed her magazine on the nightstand.

"I just wanted to say, *umm*," I hesitated.

"You just wanted to say *umm* what?" she pressed.

"That, *umm*..."

"Say what's on your mind." She tapped the empty space on the bed next to her. "Come over here. I won't bite. When Tasha first got here, this used to be her favorite spot."

I crawled onto Ms. Glo's bed and into Tasha's favorite spot. Ms. Glo draped an arm over my shoulder, and although I felt tense, like I needed to get a grip and walk away, I felt safe. Like this was where I was supposed to be.

Kamari was back to rolling across the foot of the bed.

I said, "I just wanted to say, thank you for lookin' out for me and Kamari."

"You don't have to thank me for that. That's what I'm here for. Although I should not have lied to your case-worker. I don't want you or Tasha to ever think that lying is okay. But at the same time, I didn't want you to think it was you against the world."

"I just thought because I messed up, that was it for me."

"No, life isn't like that. Family isn't about throwing you away after one mistake. *Mmph*, and besides, I was sixteen before. And if I told you some of the things I did, you wouldn't believe it."

"Like what?" I smiled, not able to imagine Ms. Glo being any different than she was right now.

"Oh, baby, I used to be boy crazy. Talk back to my parents, fight, run away, until I got hungry and had to go home. And I did a few other things that you don't need to know." She laughed.

"Is that why you wanted to have a home like this?" I asked.

"I wanted to make a difference. My son was grown and off with his own family. And I felt like I had love I could give to other kids. Kids who needed a home."

"Like me." I yawned.

"Like you, Sleepy Head." She smiled.

I lay my head on her shoulder and said, "Before I was locked up, I used to live with my grandmother. Well, she wasn't my grandmother; she was my brothers' and sister's grandmother, but I called her Nana. And she was a trip. She used to let me know e'ryday that she could call the state at any time to come and get me and my baby."

"I know that had to hurt you," Ms. Glo said.

"It made me feel so angry. I used to be so mad at the world. Didn't want anybody to say anything to me. Didn't even want people lookin' my way. I just felt trapped. Like the days, weeks, months, and seasons were passin'. But e'rything for me was still the same. Stale. Miserable. Just messed up."

"How do you feel now?"

I stared off into space, sorted through my thoughts, smiled, and said, "I feel like maybe e'rybody is not all bad." I closed my eyes, givin' in to an overwhelming need to curl up and sleep. "Yeah," I said, "I feel like maybe somethin' good might come out of this after all."

28

Rump Shaker

From the moment I walked into College Park Roller Skating Disco, I knew it was e'rything a fly time was s'posed to be. The DJ was ill, the crowd was hyped, and the place was packed.

J. J. Fad's "Supersonic" pumped through the speakers as me and Tasha walked over to the skate rental booth, handed the chubby dude behind the counter our tickets and collected our skates for the night.

"You ever been skating, Yvette?" Tasha asked, as we sat down on a red plastic bench and laced our skates.

"Well, not in a roller skating rink, but me and my cousin, Isis, used to skate through the hood all the time, especially when her brother paid us twenty dollars to keep an eye on his corner boys. We would happily skate through the block, on our way to the candy lady's house, or to get some weed, or to lick off the bodega for some jelly bracelets and a *Right On!* magazine."

Tasha laughed. "That sounds like the bomb time!"

"It was." I continued. "One time, I was about eleven, maybe twelve, and these down-south boys moved in on Face and K-Rock's—that's Isis's brother and his friend's—territory. So Face and K-Rock paid me and Isis a hunn'id dollars to put on our skates, scope the block, peep where the down-south boys kept their stashes, and watch their movements."

Tasha's eyes opened wide. "Y'all did that?"

I smiled, feelin' proud. "Yeah, we did that. You and me both know the streets is not a game. And you can't just show up on the scene and take over somebody else's block. Nah, it don't work like that."

"Not at all. So, don't stop there. What happened after that? 'Cause I know somebody got their wig snatched back."

"Yeah. Isis and her brother robbed them cats."

"Isis? I thought y'all were the same age?"

"Yeah, we are. But that don't mean we was ever kids. In Da Bricks, ain't no kids. Isis knew how to pop off, how to fight, and how to bust a cap like a man." I smiled. "Her mother and father taught her that."

"Word?"

"Word. But after Isis and Face robbed the down-south dudes, those dudes retaliated by killin' Isis's li'l brother, Schooly. E'rything fell apart after that."

"Dang. That's messed up." Tasha shook her head. "You miss Isis?"

I hesitated and my mind unexpectedly wandered into

thoughts about the good times me and Isis once had. Then I remembered she was one of the reasons my rep was ruined. "Hell, no, I don't miss her. Forget Isis." I laced my skates and stood up. "There go Reesie and Ebony." I pointed.

"Let's go meet 'em," Tasha said, and we skated to the center of the rink, beneath the spinning and mirrored disco ball, shoulders bouncin' and feet movin' to a funky beat.

"Y'all look cute," I said to Reesie and Ebony as I stood back and snapped my fingers.

"'Cause that's what we do." Reesie smiled. "Y'all fly too."

"Heyyyy! Fa'sho!" Tasha did a quick Running Man dance to show her approval.

Ebony smiled. "Y'all see how we rockin' the same thing? And we didn't even plan it."

We stood back and took in each other's outfits. We all wore oversized sweatshirts that hung off one shoulder. Mine was electric green; Tasha wore hot pink. Reesie's was fire red; and Ebony rocked neon orange. Each of our sweatshirts was paired with white stirrup pants.

"That's 'cause lovers of hotness think alike," Tasha said. "Amen!" Me and Tasha slapped high five.

I said to Ebony. "It's good to see you, homie. How are you feelin'?"

She wiped invisible sweat from her brow. "Better. I don't know what I ate at that party, but I was down for the count. For real."

"These two were straight buggin'. They thought..." I took in Reesie's and Tasha's don't-say-another-word faces, and I didn't.

"We were just worried, that's all," Tasha said.

"We're glad you're better." Reesie danced in her skates.

"Me, too!" Ebony agreed.

"Set it off I suggest y'all!," blasted through the speakers.

"Oh, hold up. Wait a minute. This is my jam!" Tasha said.

"Nope," I replied, "this is all of our jam!" And we all grooved. Actually, the whole spot was lit.

Skate teams did poppin' routines. Even a few old heads was bustin' it out. Then there was us, whoppin', bouncin', break dancin', doin' the Runnin' Man, the whop, splits, and even showin' off an ole school hustle, all on skates.

I saw a few cuties checkin' us out, and for a minute, I could've sworn I saw Li'l Herman in the mix.

I stopped skating and stood still enough to grab Tasha by the arm and whisper in her ear, "Did you invite Li'l Herman here?"

She frowned, then whispered back, "Heck no. What, I look desperate to you? That boy will never get another chance with me. He could be on fire and I wouldn't even spit on him!"

I rolled my eyes 'cause I'd heard that before and knew it was a lie. *"Umm-hmm.* Yeah. Okay."

"Why'd you ask me that?"

"I thought I saw him at the concession stand. Anyway, that doesn't matter. What matters is my how tight the DJ is!"

We waved our arms in the air and returned to groovin' around the rink. The DJ played L'Trimm's "Cars That Go Boom."

We danced and skated until we were all exhausted. The four of us rolled over to the concession stand. Each of us grabbed a burger, an order of fries to split, and fountain sodas that were a mix of Cherry Coke, Sprite, and orange.

"So, Ebony," Reesie said. "What's up with that li'l choco-late tenderoni you kicked it to at the party the other night?"

"I talked to him last night, girl!" Ebony said, givin' Reesie a high five. "We talked until the sun came up about every-thing." Her eyes scanned all of us. "I think he might be the one, y'all. I think his last name 'bout to change."

"That's wassup!" Tasha said, excited. Then she sipped her soda.

Reesie opened a mustard pack, squeezed it over her burger, and said, "That's real kind of you, Tasha...consid-ering."

We all look confused. "Huh?" I asked, reachin' for a fry. "What's real kind? And considering what?"

Reesie took a bite of her burger, then said—with a mouth full—"It's real kind of Tasha to be happy for Ebony." She licked mustard from the right corner of her mouth. "Considering Li'l Herman used her like a stamp."

Tasha was livid. "Excuse you! You always goin' two steps too far. For your information, Li'l Herman didn't use me! So don't try to play me. 'Cause I know you don't want me to tell everybody how you came to me crying 'cause you found out Jerelle was only fourteen."

"Fourteen!" Me and Ebony screamed simultaneously.

"How'd you find that out?" Ebony asked.

Tasha answered, "When his twelve-year-old girlfriend called Reesie's phone and told her that if she called her man one more time, she was gon' whup her old ass!"

Reesie took another bite of her burger and said, "See, this is how rumors get started. 'Cause first of all, Tasha, you're loud and wrong. One: I wasn't crying. I have bad al-lergies. Two: Jerelle is fourteen and a half. And three: That wasn't his girlfriend. He called and said he broke up with her. And anyway, why are you beefing with me? I'm on your side. I'm ya homegirl. So don't try and put me on blast. That ain't right. I would never tear the drawls off your business like that. And you know I'm the main one who would watch you jump on Li'l Herman and make sure don't nobody else get in it. And if you want to, you really could steal on him now, especially since he's comin' this way."

Tasha's eyes bucked like a deer caught in the headlights. "What?" She sucked in a breath, clearly tryin' to fight off a smile. "What do you mean Li'l Herman is coming this way? He's here?"

"I knew that was him," I said, and just as I motioned to turn around, Tasha grabbed my arm.

"No. Don't look. He might see you," she said.

"So? I don't care if he sees me."

"I care."

"Why?"

"'Cause I don't want him to see me."

"Why not?" I asked.

"'Cause we gotta look busy. I don't need him thinking I'm moping around and missing him. 'Cause I'm not. I barely even think about that boy. He ain't my type no way."

I paused, 'cause obviously this chick forgot that we lived together, and just last night I'd listened to her, for half of the night, whine about how she really liked him, how he was almost her man of the week, and how she didn't know if she'd ever look at homeroom the same. I guess all of that slipped her mind.

"So what do you suggest?" I said. "When he comes over here, we should act, what, 'sleep?"

Reesie snapped her fingers. "That's a bomb idea. We could do that."

"We gon' act asleep in the skatin' rink?" I twisted my lips. "With all this noise and loud music? Seriously? Be for real."

"Let's just act like he doesn't exist," Ebony said.

"Better idea." I gave Ebony a high five.

We all turned around and resumed eating our food and talkin' about Ebony's new boo, Black Conscious.

Li'l Herman walked over to our table, then took his fist and knocked on the edge. "Hey, wassup?" he asked.

Not one response. Screw him.

"Hey y'all," Li'l Herman said.

Nothing.

"That's real foul, yo," Li'l Herman said with an attitude. "I can't believe this. After I got all four of y'all into the concert *and* took you to the after-party."

Reesie batted her lashes. "Oh, that was so petty, *Herman*."

Tasha looked over at Li'l Herman. "So what? You took us to the concert and? What? You want a cookie? You need a prize for that? You tried to play me with your homies, and now you think me and my homegirls should talk to you? Boy boo. Run along."

Li'l Herman shook his head. "Tasha, it wasn't even like that."

Reesie said, "Lies. And deceit. We heard you, Li'l Herman."

"Yo, yo, yo!" came from behind us. We all turned around and looked. It was Lottie.

Reesie's eyes lit up with delight and she mouthed to me, "There goes your man."

I mouthed back, "No he's not."

"Wassup, good people?" Lottie walked over to the table.

He didn't light my fire like Brooklyn, but he was a cutie and his gear was fly too: Guess jeans, a white tee, and an 8-ball jacket. "Hey, ladies." He waved, then he looked directly at me and said, "Hey, stranger, wassup?"

"Nothin'." I smiled.

Lottie looked over at Li'l Herman and gave him a pound. "Cuz! What's good, homie? You hangin' out with your girl and her crew?"

"Negative," Reesie said.

Tasha added, "This is my crew. But I am not his girl."

Lottie chuckled. "Yo, cut my cousin some slack."

"For real," Li'l Herman said.

Tasha pointed and shook her index finger. "Oh, don't do that, Li'l Herman. Don't play victim. You know what you did."

Li'l Herman huffed. "Look, I'm sorry, Tasha. My bad. I never thought you'd really go out with me and when you said yes, I was so excited that I did somethin' stupid. I'm asking you to forgive me though...'cause I miss you."

"Lies." Reesie grabbed Tasha's hand and locked into her eyes. "Look at me. He don't miss you, girl. Don't fall for it. Don't. He just wanna get in yo' drawls and brag about yo' pop-pop-get-it-get to his team. Don't do it, girl. Don't."

"Yo," Li'l Herman said to Reesie, "would you mind your business?"

Reesie snapped, "This is my business, Herman! And get me? I ain't no dog!"

"Then you need to stop tryna sick me!"

Reesie rolled her eyes. "You are so freakin' corny. What you gon' do, cry next? You really need to grow up and stop wearing panties."

Me and Ebony shot Reesie a look.

"You lucky Tasha is my girl!" Reesie said, then resumed eating her food.

Li'l Herman continued. "Tasha, if you'll accept my apology, I'll do anything to make it up to you."

"Awl, man," Lottie said, looking over at Tasha, "you gotta give my cuzo another chance. He's a changed man."

"For real, I am," Li'l Herman begged.

"You ain't change that fast." Tasha rolled her eyes.

Li'l Herman popped his collar. "Girl, don't you know they call me Superman? All I gotta do is go into a phone booth and boom, I'm somebody new."

Tasha tried to fight off her laugh, but couldn't.

Reesie smacked her lips and said to Tasha, "Superman by any other name is still Clark Kent. So nothin' he does will make you Lois Lane. Don't fall for that. Make him sweat you, girl."

"Reesie," I said sternly.

"What?" She shrugged. "I'm just sayin'." She picked up her cup and shook the ice. "Know what, I'ma mind my business. People don't appreciate it when you keepin' it real."

I could tell Tasha wanted to smile, but with her pride and Reesie's constant interruptions, she wouldn't dare set her heart free, not at this table anyway.

So before she could say *no* just to impress us, I said, "Li'l Herman, she gon' give you this one last chance. And that's it."

Tasha looked at me like I had lost my mind. "No, you didn't just make up with him for me. I ain't thinking about that boy."

I twisted my lips. "You need to quit."

Tasha sighed, hesitated, soaked in a thought, then said, "Okay, Li'l Herman, but if you mess up again..."

"I'm not gon' mess up." He smiled. "I promise. So can I get another chance to take you out?"

"Yeah, I guess," Tasha answered. "And you can start by taking us home, so we don't have to take the bus."

"Y'all ready now? I'll take y'all home," Li'l Herman said, way too excited.

Lottie looked over at me and said, "That's too bad. I wanted to kick it to you a little longer, shawtie."

"Maybe next time," I replied as we slid out of the booth.

"Or maybe she can ride with you and you can take her home," Tasha said to Lottie.

"I'd love to take you home," Lottie said.

I shot Tasha a look. "I don't think..."

"And she would love it too," Tasha responded. "So, yeah, you can take her home." She playfully pushed me towards him.

Lottie caught me, and with full confidence, placed an arm around my waist. He continued. "Yvette, what do you think about that? I hear your girl talkin', but I need a yes from you."

"*Umm*...Yeah," I said, taking a step back and letting his arm fall off my waist. "Yeah, maybe. I guess. Sure, you can take me home."

29

Faker

I had to admit that despite me really not wanting to be here with Lottie, his car was stupid fresh and his system was bananas!

He drove a gleaming 1985 silver Mercedes coupe with a knockin' Bose stereo system that rocked the Norfolk blocks we rode through, turnin' ordinary people who'd sat on their porches when we'd first entered their block into standing spectators by the time we'd turned the corner.

The D.O.C.'s latest hit blasted out the tinted, deep purple windows.

Lottie nodded his head to the beat. He also had one hand on the steering wheel and the other stretched over the back of my seat.

Maybe... I need to chill. Just relax. I mean, he's ai'ight. Maybe he's more than that.

I glanced over at him and flashed him a smile. He shot me one back.

He's a cutie. Plus, he seems to be doing his thing. His

car is dope. He got his own crib. And he gotta have some money. But still...he ain't Brooklyn.

You're actin' real crazy behind a dude you don't even kick it with. Brooklyn is probably off with some baby bird, coupled up. So chill wit' Lottie and forget Brooklyn.

Lottie turned the music down and said, "A nickel for your thoughts."

I laughed. "You better come up with a dollar for each of these thoughts. 'Cause you will not get too far with a nickel, boo."

He smiled. "A dollar, huh? Those thoughts better be the bomb then."

"The bomb, like what?"

"Like, you better be thinkin' about how you checkin' for me. How you gon' let me take you out. Wine and dine you. How fine, fly, and correct I am." He pulled up to a red light, then turned his head and looked me in the eyes. "That we gon' chill on a regular basis. I'm hoping those are your thoughts." He smiled and his gold grill lit up the car.

Boy, please. No. I am not about to be chillin' with you and them teeth on the regular. Plus, I'm tired of old men.

I shook my head. "So what happened to my dollars? Or are your guesses the cheap way out?"

Lottie laughed. "Come on, Li'l Ma, you have to clue me in on something."

"Okay, I'll give this thought away: I think you're okay."

"Okay?" he said, as the light turned green and he returned his attention to the street. "Do you know who I am? And how many chicks are checkin' for me, and you're tellin' me I'm okay? What? You got a fever or something? Why are you dissin' me?"

"I'm not dissin' you. All I'm sayin' is that I have to get to know you and see what your winin' and dinin' consists of. 'Cause I don't wanna be a part of no five-dollar-who-gon-get-the-drawls bet."

"What?" He laughed, making a left turn, and driving slowly down a weeping willow–lined street, where all of the houses were McMansions, framed with sprawling lawns and circular driveways. "Five-dollar-panty-bet, what is that?"

"Just some stupid bet the boys made in school."

"See, that's the difference between me and them. I'm not a boy. I'ma twenty-five-year-old man."

"Age ain't nothin' but a number. How you act will let me know if you're a man or not. And anyway, like I said, I gotta get to know you first before I say if we can chill on a regular. Plus, I'm just movin' down here, just gettin' to know people."

"Well, the only way you're going to get to know me is if you let me take you out on a date." He paused. "Unless you feel like me bein' twenty-five is a problem for you. Most chicks your age like older dudes. Plus, you already know who I am and what I bring to the table. Trust me, when the girls in your school find out you're seeing me, they gon' be sweatin' you, dyin' to be a part of your crew."

Oh he is really feelin' himself.

I said, "I don't really trust girls all that well so, truth-fully, I don't need any more chicks in my crew. The three I hang with is more than enough. And I'm not most girls my age, 'cause half of 'em wouldn't even know how to survive half of the things I've been through. So, it's gon' take more than you promotin' parties to impress me."

He scrunched his brow. "Cut me some slack."

"That must be your line of the day. And anyway, I am cuttin' you plenty of slack. You couldn't handle me if I was all the way on."

"Is that so?"

"Maybe." I smiled. "I'm curious to know somethin', though."

"What's that?"

"How long have you been promoting concerts and parties?"

"Two, almost three, years now."

"And you make enough to sport a Benz?"

"Yeah. You see I'm whippin' it."

"I see that, which is why I'm askin'."

"Yeah, people e'rywhere get at me when they want their parties to be stupid. I started promoting when I lived in New York."

"Why'd you leave New York? That's the party capital."

"'Cause I got the juice."

Boy, please.

He continued. "And Virginia was calling my name."

"That's what's up," I said sarcastically. "The whole state?"

"The whole state. They know how I do it. I'm the reason the hip-hop scene is alive and poppin' down here. You like hip-hop?"

"I love hip-hop. I used to break dance and e'rything."

"Stop playin'." Lottie laughed.

"I ain't playin'."

"Say word," Lottie said, impressed.

"Word," I said. *I need to chill and stop being so uptight.* I continued. "Check it; when I was home in Newark, I wanted to be an MC."

He chuckled. "An MC. And what was gon' be your name? Shortie?"

"Funny. Although, that would be kind of fresh." I did a mini approval dance in my seat. "But my name would've been Scratch MC. 'Cause I scratch too and beatbox." I cupped my hand over my mouth and hit him with some sounds.

"Ai'ight, ai'ight. I see you. Yo," he said seriously. "You know I could get you into the studio. I produce too. Maybe we could lay down some tracks. We can head over to the studio now if you want."

"Nah, I have to get home. Maybe the next time, though."

"So it'll be a next time? Is that a promise?"

"Can I bring my girls with me?" I asked.

"*Umm* . . . yeah . . . sure." Lottie hesitated, looking in his rearview mirror strangely.

"What's wrong?" I asked and flipped the mirrored visor down. There was a cop car behind us. "They followin' you or something?"

"I think so," he said. "They've been behind me for a minute."

"Maybe we need to get out of this neighborhood."

"Maybe so." Lottie took another glance in the rearview mirror before making a right turn, then a quick left. "They still behind me, yo," he said with a slight tinge of panic in his voice. "Shit." He groaned, as the cop car's sirens flashed and blue lights lit up the otherwise dark street.

"Damn." Lottie shifted in his seat, taking two bags of weed from his pocket, and shoving it into my hands. "Here. Put this in your purse."

Shocked, I tossed the weed back into his lap. "Hell, no! I don't know what you think this is!"

"Listen, I just need you to put this in your bag," he said, watching the cop in the rearview mirror.

"That's yours and you need to hold it."

"I can't. I'm a felon."

"A felon?"

"Listen, you're a minor; if you take this weed, all you gon' get is a slap on the wrist. And they gon' let you go tonight, but me, that's gon' be a violation of my parole."

"Parole?! I knew you were doing more than promotin' parties. Yo! I'ma kill Tasha!"

Lottie continued. "I ain't goin' back to jail, yo."

"And me either!" I snapped.

Lottie peeked back into the mirror. "The cop's comin'." He slid the weed under his seat and mumbled, "I can't believe you gon' play me like that! You know how many chicks would love to be in your spot, including your little girlfriends."

"Check it; if you got another ho whose gon' take some charges for you, then you need to call 'em. 'Cause I ain't the one. I don't even know you like that! You must be crazy!"

"Be quiet, I said. Here he comes!"

"You tell me to be quiet? That's called immunity, which is what the state gon' offer me when I tell on yo' fake, promotin', wanna-be gangster-behind. Word is bond. You lucky I don't have my blade on me right now!"

"Shut up!"

"Don't tell me shut up! Mess around and get white-chalked!"

The cop pressed one hand on the car's hood and the other on his gun holster.

Lottie rolled the window down and said, like he didn't
have a care in the world, "Hello, Officer."

*I knew I should not have let him take me home! I knew
it! Dear God, please get me out of this.*

"What seems to be the problem?" Lottie asked, the left
side of his mouth twitchin' and beads of sweat formin' on
his forehead.

*Your corny behind is the problem! Tryna sound all
cool, calm, and collected, but I betchu in the middle of
your whitey tighties is a fresh skid mark. Punk!*

"Good evening, folks." The officer looked over at me
and nodded, then looked back over to Lottie. "I need your
license and registration, please."

"Sure, sir." Lottie reached into the glove compartment,
retrieved his paperwork, and handed it to the officer.
"Here you are. Can you please tell me what the problem
is, sir?"

*You're problem number one, and the weed under your
seat is problem number two.*

The officer looked at Lottie's license and said, "Just
give me a moment, Mr. Clark; sit tight. I'll be right back
to explain the situation." He walked away and over to his
patrol car.

*Dear God. Jesus. Mary. Joseph. Oprah. Michael Jack-
son. Somebody. If you get me outta this, I will never again
be bothered with this joker.*

I said to Lottie, while rockin' nervously in my seat, "I
promise you, son, your name might be Lottie Clark right
now, but when the cop comes over here, if he has to
search this car and he finds your weed, you will be goin' to
jail. And the soap-droppin' crew gon' be waitin' for you. I

can promise you that. And Cell Block D will be callin' you Loretta Clink-Clink."

"If you don't stop running your mouth and shut up your name gon' be Get Out And Walk."

Oh no, he didn't!

"Okay, son," the officer said as he returned and handed Lottie his paperwork. "I stopped you because you have a broken taillight."

"A broken taillight?" Lottie said, relieved.

"Yeah, and you need to get that fixed as soon as possible."

"I will, sir. Thank you."

The officer tipped his cap, and a few minutes later he was gone.

Lottie drove down the block and said, "Little girl, I swear, if you say another word, I'm pulling over and you're getting the hell out!"

Screech! What?! "Stop the press. You got me all the way messed up. And 'little girl'? I wasn't a little girl when your old behind was tryin' to be my man."

"Tryna be your man? Ain't nobody checkin' for you like that! You ain't even down, so you could never be one of my chicks. Obviously, you don't know who I am!"

I slammed my hand on the dashboard. "Know who you are?! Who are you? Are you anything more than a wet butt-crack? Stupid? Whack? Dumb as hell? 'Cause from where I'm sittin', that's exactly who you are. But I can tell you what I'm not. I'm not some weak li'l broad who's shot out over you. You better come correct, 'cause I ain't the one. Especially if you think I should not only catch a case for you, but believe you'd really show up at the police station for me; boy, please. Been there. Done that. And I ain't goin' back. Now this ride has ended; pull over and let me out! Now!" I pointed at an upcoming bus stop.

Lottie kept driving and passed the bus stop.

"Oh you not gon' pull over! Oh, okay, watch this!" I opened the door, inches from sideswiping a parked car.

"Yo, chill!" Lottie swerved and then yanked into an empty space, slammin' on brakes.

I jerked forward, then snapped, "Now carry yo' knock-off, hustlin' behind somewhere! S'pose to be a promoter; how about you promote my back, 'cause that's all you gon' see of me! Fake weed-sellin' sucker! Chump!" I got out of Lottie's car and slammed the door.

He pulled off and just when I thought things couldn't get any worse, the evening sky opened up and rain poured all...over...me.

My hair was drenched, and I knew for sure by the time I found my way home I was gon' be sick.

I was blocks from the bus stop and even still I had no idea what bus to take. There were no pay phones in sight, so I couldn't even call Ms. Glo.

I noticed a dark brown Chevette riding along side of me and just as I was about to cross the street to get away from this mysterious freak, the car pulled over and the passenger side window rolled down.

I squinted. "Brooklyn?"

"Bricks?" Brooklyn hesitated. "What are you doing out here?"

Thank God!

"Get in." Brooklyn reached over and pulled up the lock.

I was soaking wet when I got into the car. "Boy, I am so dang happy to see you!" I let out a sigh of relief.

"That's 'cause I'm the man." He smiled, wiping the rain from my eyes with the backs of his thumbs.

I laughed. "Any other time I would tell you how whack it is to ride your own sack, but right now I'ma have to agree with you, you're the man." I shot him a soggy high five.

He flicked the excess water from his hand. "Yo, why are you out here just walkin' around in the rain? Is that what y'all do up north? 'Cause down here we call that a li'l crazy."

I chuckled. "Whatever. I'm trying to get home. And, anyway, the question is, where are you comin' from?"

"You're never supposed to answer a question with a question."

"So, what you're sayin' is, you want me to answer your question, but you don't wanna answer mine."

"No, what I'm sayin' is, I asked you first. But if you must know, I was chillin' with a friend," he said.

"Who? The yuck-muck from the other night?"

"Now why you calling names? Didn't I tell you before to watch your mouth. And don't worry about who it was; just know it was a friend. Now, your turn." He put the car in gear and took off down the street.

I looked him over and did my best to rate his trust meter; he ranked in between highly trustworthy and maybe not so much. I took a chance. "If I tell you, you better not laugh and you better not tell a soul. 'Cause I'm pissed off to the max. and I don't think it's funny."

"I won't laugh."

"Pinky swear?" I held my pinky out.

He frowned. "I'm not 'bout to pinky swear with you. I'm a man. I don't do that."

"Well, if you don't pinky swear, I'm not gon' be able to tell you."

"Why?"

"'Cause that's the only way I'ma know if you're able to keep your mouth closed."

Brooklyn shook his head. "Don't be tellin' nobody I'm up in here pinky swearin'." He locked his pinky with mine.

"Bet," I said as he continued driving. "So it all started when me, Tasha, and Reesie was at the skatin' rink. We ran into Li'l Herman, who was beggin' Tasha like a fiend needin' to cop."

Brooklyn laughed, as he made a right turn. "Chill. Don't dog my boy like that."

"You can never be dogged by the truth. Anyhow, Lottie also happened to be at the skating rink."

"Lottie." Brooklyn frowned. "Your boyfriend?"

"He is not my boyfriend."

"That's what your mouth says. I hear you talkin'. But I also see you out here chillin' with him." He stopped at a red light.

"You gon' let me tell the story or you got it from here?"

"I'm listening."

"Prove it."

"How?" The light changed to green.

"Prove it by being quiet. Now, as I was sayin', Lottie asked could he take me home, and I told him yeah. And at first the ride was okay. We laughed a little. Talked; you know, we kicked it. Then the police stepped in."

"The police?"

"The police. And they pulled him over."

"What?" Brooklyn's eyes popped wide open.

"Yup. And this dude had two bags of weed on him."

"Weed! Say word."

"Yoooooo, word to the tenth power!"

"Then he announces he's a felon, on parole!" I told Brooklyn e'rything, not leaving out a single detail, including how I told Lottie his name was gon' be Loretta Clink-Clink.

Brooklyn laughed so hard that, although we were only down the street from where I lived, he had to pull over. "Yo, you straight flipped on him."

I gave Brooklyn a high five. "Heck yes, I did. My freedom is not a game."

Brooklyn shook his head. "Now see, had you gon' out with me, I would've hooked you up with some Burger King and we would've driven down to the beach and chilled with a Luther cassette in the backdrop."

"Oh, really?" I said. "Burger King. How romantic. 'Cause the Big Mac is the illest."

"It's the Whopper. And you know it's nothin' better than a burger and an order of fries by candle light," Brooklyn said as he drove up the street and parked in front of Ms. Glo's house.

I smiled and said, "Oh, so we gon' have candles? Now that might make me say yes."

"Of course you gon' say yes, 'cause it's fresh."

"Oh really, is that why I'ma say yes?"

"Yeah, plus you're tired of running from me."

Now that was the truth. I was tired of runnin' from him.

I grew silent. Mainly because I knew I could no longer push him away, and I didn't want to. But then again, when I was willing to confess my feelings to him, he showed up at the party with some dame on his arms, so suppose he now has a girlfriend. I'm not about to pour my heart out and make myself look dumb.

"Do you have a girl?" I asked.

"What?" He looked taken aback. "Where did that come from? No, I don't have a girl."

"So what was up with ole girl at the party?"

"I told you, I met her at the party and I left her there."

"Looked like a full-on date to me."

"You should stop assuming, and anyway, why are you buggin'? I'm the one who should be looking at you sideways. I've been askin' you out, and you've been playin' me, I guess, for ole boy."

"That is not true."

"Looks that way to me. *Mmph*, maybe I ain't thug enough for you. Maybe you need a dude who's two seconds from sending you to jail."

"Now who should stop assuming?"

"I'm just calling it how I see it."

"Well, you need glasses. And, for your information, at the after-party I was ready to step to you and be like, 'I'm feelin' you. I think you're cute. And maybe we should hang out sometimes.'"

"What stopped you?"

I twisted my lips. "You knooooow what stopped me! You and your new boo."

"I told you I met her at the party." He shrugged. "No big deal."

"It was a big deal to me."

"Okay, that was then; this is now. It's nobody here but me and you, so what's your excuse? Do you like me?"

"I think . . ."

"And tell the truth, in one word."

"Brooklyn..."

He leaned into me and placed his forehead against mine. "Yes or no."

I looked into his eyes and all I wanted to do was kiss him and say *yes* in my best Pam Grier voice, but I couldn't, so I said, "I never really dated a boy like you before."

He lifted his forehead from mine. "What does that mean?"

"It means I'm not like some innocent little girl, who's moved to the south for fresh air. Like, I don't have a choice but to be here."

"Why don't you have a choice?"

I did my best to rate his trust meter again. It was the same, so I took another chance. "Well, you may not know this, but I have a two-year-old little girl."

"Really? Okay," he said, and I couldn't tell if he was surprised or indifferent.

I continued, "Yeah, and we couldn't live in Jersey any longer because I kept getting into trouble."

"What kind of trouble?"

"I had a fight and I sliced a girl in her face. We used to be friends and we had an argument. Long story. I mean, I wish I'd handled it differently. But I didn't. And here I am. Sentenced to get my life right or bust."

"So that's your story, huh?"

"Most of it." I shrugged.

"Bricks, none of us are perfect."

"I know, but..."

"Look, from the first day I saw you, I was checkin' for you and wanted to know who you were."

"And now that you know?"

"I want to get to know you even better. What you need me to do, write you a note?"

I laughed. "No. I don't need a note."

"So wassup with us?"

Us? Did he just say us? *Breathe. Breathe. Relax.* I moved in closer to him, slid my arms around his neck, and said, "I think we should give us a chance. But I don't know where to start."

"With a kiss," he said, and his heated tongue eased into my mouth and did a sweet dance with mine.

"That did not look like Lottie," Tasha said, scaring the heck out of me as I walked in the door.

"It wasn't." I tossed her a smile and walked to my room. "Now good night."

"Good night? Heifer, I know you don't think you're about to go to bed. Oh hellll, no! You got some explaining to do."

30

Top Billin'

1990

If ever thought you was chilled, but yo' car didn't have a boomin' system, you was a chump.

Straight up.

Cross Colours was on the rise.

Air Jordans was the illest.

Ice Cube was America's Most Wanted.

George H. W. Bush was president.

LL Cool J wanted to knock you out.

Big Daddy Kane offered e'rybody a taste of chocolate.

Madonna was no longer a virgin.

The hustlers and the lovers had the pay phones locked down.

Two ways was the new street jones.

But if you was in love, like me, then nothin' else mattered but your sweetie.

Me and Tasha was on the porch chillin' while Ms. Glo and Kamari were in the backyard watering the garden.

"Yvette, you ever envision yourself some place like this?" Tasha asked, leaning over the banister and looking down at me.

I sat on the middle step, laid back on both elbows. I pulled in the thought of me sittin' in Da Bricks courtyard, sippin' a forty, while pushing Kamari in her umbrella stroller. "Nah, never. I used to think that all I was gon' ever do was sit somewhere on the edge wantin' to leave Newark and wantin' to stay, all at the same time."

"I feel you in that. That's how I was when I was in Compton. I could never see a way out. And I wasn't gon' put no bullet to my head and check out like that, so I knew one day that something had to change. I just didn't expect it to change after I robbed a gas station, was arrested, and sentenced to live here."

"I feel you," I said. "And when my PD told me that the prosecutor was offering me a plea bargain and I had to come to a"—I made air quotes—"Professional Parent Home, I looked at her like, trick, please."

"Me too!" Tasha said. "We are too much alike. I'm glad you're here, though, Yvette. You and Kamari."

"Me too. I just wish I didn't slice Munch's face to get here. I feel bad about that." I paused. "Do you ever wonder why some people have their family's support and love, while people like us don't have it at all."

"No, I mean, I guess I learned that you don't have to be blood to be family; sometimes water is thicker. And, as far as I'm concerned, you're my sister, Kamari is my niece, Aunty Glo is my mother, and Li'l Herman is my boo!" She pointed across the street at Li'l Herman and Brooklyn who were headed our way. Tasha continued. "So life is super sweet." She walked off the porch to meet Li'l Herman. "And fine." She gave him a peck on the lips.

"Hey, my sweet butter biscuit. My snookums," Li'l Herman said.

Tasha giggled, and I wanted to gag.

Brooklyn, who was wearing a baseball cap and had a book bag slung over his shoulder, gave me a soft wink and pointed at Tasha and his friend. "Check them out," he said. "How much you wanna bet, he's about to ask her to go with him to Feather-N-Fin?"

"How much you wanna bet she gon' say yes?" I said.

Tasha grinned, then said, "You know we can hear you two, right? And of course I'm going to say yes." She looked over at Li'l Herman. "Come on, baby, you don't even have to ask."

"Let's roll, pumpkin pie," Li'l Herman said to Tasha and grabbed her by the hand. They walked down the street to where his mother's car was parked and, a few seconds later, were on their way.

I shielded my eyes from the movin' sunray and said to Brooklyn, "What's with the backpack and the hat?"

He gave me a crooked grin, opened the backpack and pulled out a towel, which he draped over my lap, a comb and a brush, which he handed me, and a jar of yellow hair grease. He lifted his baseball cap, revealing his wild mane. "I need you to hook this up. My sister's buggin'. She wanted to charge me ten dollars."

"Well, I charge twenty."

"How you gon' charge your man twenty dollars? You know how foul that sounds?"

"*Umm*, excuse you, sir. I don't remember you asking me to be your girl?"

"What? We've been kicking it for three months."

"My point exactly. We've been kicking it."

"So is that your way of saying you don't want to braid my hair?"

"I didn't say that."

"Is that a yes?"

"How do you know I can even braid hair?" I asked, as I motioned for him to sit between my knees.

It was hard to maintain my composure being so close to Brooklyn. The warmth of his arms draped over my legs and the beauty of him laying his head on my thigh made me want to melt.

But I didn't. Instead, I kissed him on his forehead and began to braid his hair.

"So, Bricks, I want to ask you something," he said.

"What's that?"

"What's up with you and Kamari's father? Where is he at?"

I hesitated. "Why are you asking me that?"

"Because I never hear you mention him or say anything at all about him."

"He's in Jersey."

"Does he see Kamari?"

"No." I shook my head, gathering a section of Brooklyn's hair, separating it into three parts, intertwining it between my fingers and into a thin cornrow. I moved onto another section of his hair.

"Why not?" Brooklyn asked.

"You really wanna know?"

"Yeah."

"Because he's a thirty-year-old junkie in the street. And he doesn't care about me or Kamari. And the best thing I could do for the both of us was to get as far away from him as possible."

"Thirty years old?" Brooklyn turned his head and lifted his eyes toward me.

"Would you turn back around and keep your head still? And yes, thirty. He might even be older than that."

"Did you know how old he was when you started messing around with him?"

"Yeah, I knew, but at the time I didn't see anything wrong with it."

"How could you not see anything wrong with that?"

"My life was not like yours. Like how you have your mother and father. Your sister. And you all live together, like a family should. I didn't have that."

"What was your life like?"

"I lived here, there, and everywhere. I didn't know my father, and my mother was a junkie so she never stayed anywhere for long. Before I got into trouble and had to come and live here, I never thought a life like this was possible." I paused, praying he didn't ask me exactly what that meant. There was no way I was going to tell him that Ms. Glo was something like a foster home. He didn't need to know that. "I never thought I'd just be regular. Well, a regular teen with a baby. No worries, nobody callin' me names, stressing me about bringing money into the house. Have an allowance. This life here is, like, amazing."

"Damn, Bricks, you had it hard."

"Yeah, I did. Does that change how you feel about me? Like, what do you think?"

"I think you should write a book."

"Funny." I playfully popped him on the side of his neck with the comb.

"Hey, watch it." Brooklyn laughed, then said, "I like you a lot. And I want you to be my girl."

I hugged him around his neck.

"Is that a yes?" he said.

"Of course it's a yes!"

"Great, so maybe now you can give me a kiss and stop choking me."

31

It Never Rains in Southern California

"**O**h, this is my jam!" Tasha said as we rocked to the beat of Tony! Toni! Tone's "It Never Rains (in Southern California)." We were at Li'l Herman's basement birthday party. He'd invited everybody in the school, and judging from the crowd, everybody showed up.

I looked over at Tasha, Reese, and Ebony and said, "I'm going to get my baby, Brooklyn, and get my slow drag on."

"Me too," Tasha said. "I'm going to get Li'l Herman so we can grind in the corner."

Reesie smirked. "With y'all nasty selves, don't get pregnant."

"Whatever," Tasha said. "Come on, Yvette. Reesie is just mad, as usual."

Me and Tasha walked over to the juice bar where Li'l Herman stood kickin' it with some of his boys from school. "Baby," Tasha whined, "I wanna dance."

Li'l Herman's face lit up. "Well, whatever, my baby wants, she's gon' get."

All I could do was laugh. These two were a mess. I scanned the crowd at the bar then said to Li'l Herman, "Where's Brooklyn?"

"I'm not sure. He was just standing here. Maybe he went to the bathroom."

"Maybe," I said, so low I was pretty much talking to myself.

Li'l Herman grabbed Tasha by the waist and led her to the middle of the dance floor.

I waited by the bar and swayed back and forth to the music for a few minutes. No Brooklyn.

Two songs ended and the DJ had mixed a third one in.

I grew tired of waiting, so I walked over to the bathroom. The door was open and the bathroom was empty.

I walked up the stairs and into the living room. That's when I noticed the front door was open.

Maybe he had to get something out of his car.

I walked over to the screen door, ready to push it open. I heard voices and jumped back.

I knew one voice belonged to Brooklyn and the other belonged to a girl. I just couldn't tell by her voice who she was.

"Brooklyn," she said, "I can't believe you showed up here with her!"

Nervousness filled my stomach, and I sucked in a quick breath.

"You buggin', Alesha," Brooklyn said, annoyed. "That's my girlfriend. Who did you expect me to bring? You? We're not together."

"You owe me and this baby a chance at being a family!" Alesha said, and my heart dropped to my feet.

Baby? What does she mean baby?

Whose baby?

"You probably didn't even tell her I'm pregnant," she spat.

"Do you even know if you're pregnant?" Brooklyn demanded to know.

"My period didn't come for three months!"

"I was with you once since we broke up and that was it. How do I even know it's mine?!"

Alesha sobbed. "I don't believe you said that to me! You're the only one I've ever been with."

"How do I know that?"

"I can't believe you're saying this to me! All this for some tramp! If you don't tell her that I'm pregnant, I will!"

"Alesha," Brooklyn said. "Wait!"

"No!" she said and charged into the house. She practically knocked me down when she stormed into the living room.

"What was that about?" I said to Brooklyn as Alesha fled into the basement.

"*Umm*, nothing."

He lied to me. I can't believe he lied to me.

He continued. "What are you doing standing here?"

"I was looking for you."

"I had to get something out of my car."

Another lie.

"And bumped into the nut job, Alesha."

She might be a nut job, but your lies probably made her that way.

It was a struggle to hold myself together as I said, "My song was on and I wanted us to dance."

Brooklyn forced himself to smile. "Sure, Yvette."

Yvette? He never called me Yvette before.

"Let's go dance then." Brooklyn grabbed me by the hand and led me back to the basement and to the center of the dance floor. The DJ called last dance and Luther Vandross's "If This World Were Mine" played. We swayed quietly, both lost in our thoughts.

"You know I love you, Yvette," Brooklyn said.

I froze. Usually I could say it back, but this time I couldn't.

I just continued to dance and breathe in his scent, knowing I'd never let him get this close to me again.

"I'm ready to go," I said to Brooklyn, not wanting to stay here a moment longer.

"Why?" He looked confused.

I didn't answer that. "Are you going to take me home or do I have to call a cab?"

"A cab? Why are you trippin'?"

"Oh, now I'm trippin'?" I could feel my pressure rising. "Look, I just want to go home."

"Ai'ight," Brooklyn said. "Let's go."

Once we were in Brooklyn's car, I turned and looked out the window, doing everything I could not to cry. We rode all the way to Ms. Glo's in silence.

Brooklyn parked and said, "What's wrong with you? You've been acting funny practically all night."

"No, I haven't. Only after I spotted you with your girlfriend."

"You're my girlfriend. And I told you I had to get something out of my car."

"Stop lying."

"So you're calling me a liar now?"

"Are you lying?"

He hesitated. "What I need to lie for?"

"Exactly. And since when did you start calling me Yvette?"

"What? I can't call you Yvette?" he snapped.

"I never said that," I barked back. "And I'd appreciate it if you didn't take your attitude out on me 'cause I didn't do anything to you."

"You're right; you didn't." He paused. "I am a little upset that I told you I loved you and you didn't say a word. You didn't even say it back. So what are you trying to say—that you don't love me?"

Of course I love you. I love you so much I feel like I've loved you all of my life. And you know that!

I bit my bottom lip and sank deeper in disappointment. I could smell a set up a mile away, and I knew that Brooklyn was trying to switch things around on me and make me look like the problem, so he'd have an easy escape route. But there was no need for him to try that hard because I was about to give him one.

"Check it; you cute and all and you've been a nice li'l boyfriend, but I ain't on it like that."

"What? Li'l boyfriend?" He blinked and shot me a look.

"Yes, that's what I said."

"Yvette, you don't mean that."

"Don't tell me what I mean. I'm not stupid and I'm not shot out over you, so I know what I'm saying. You just need to accept it."

"Accept what? What exactly are you sayin'? Where is this coming from?"

"Don't question me. How about you tell me how long you cheated on me with Alesha. I know I wasn't givin' you none, but damn, you ain't have to play me like that."

"What? Cheat on you? I didn't cheat on you."

I rolled my eyes to the ceiling. More lies. "Then how did she get pregnant, Brooklyn? What are you, Joseph now, and this trick is havin' Jesus? You really need to quit lying because you're not good at it."

"Look." He took a deep breath. "Let me explain."

"You don't have to." I hopped out of the car and slammed the door.

He followed me onto the porch. "Would you just listen? I didn't cheat on you."

"So it's a miracle. The second coming?"

"No," he said, "the night I picked you up in the rain I was coming from her house."

"So that was your friend? And y'all were screwin' and you've probably been screwin', which is why she lost control and went off on me that day in the parking lot after school."

"Since we broke up, we only were in that situation once. I never cheated on you. Ever."

"Oh, is that what you call it, a situation? How whack is that? I call it sex! But whatever. How long have you known she was pregnant?"

"I don't know for sure if she's pregnant now. She told me that she hasn't had her cycle in three months. And that she was scared to tell me, but she knew that she would be showing soon and she had to tell me something."

"And when were you going to tell me?"

"I don't know, but I would've told you. I just didn't know how to tell you."

"You open your mouth and speak. Instead of me having to look for you at your boy's party and overhear the future birth announcement."

"I don't even know if it's mine," he said.

"So typical. Now you don't know if it's yours."

"I don't! And you have to believe me!"

"I don't have to believe a damn thing. All I need to do in life is stay black and die. That's it." Tears pounded the back of my eyes and an iron fist filled my throat. "I gotta go." I hopped out the car and onto the porch.

"Bricks," Brooklyn came behind me.

"It's Yvette." I snatched away. "And don't touch me."

"Bricks..."

"Look, it was fun while it lasted, but this is where I get off. I don't have time for a boyfriend anyway."

"Bricks, hear me out. Please don't do this."

"Don't tell me what to do. How about this, I'ma go take care of my baby and you go take care of yours." I rushed inside and slammed the door, shutting out the echo of him screaming my name behind me.

Ms. Glo, on the couch, looked startled. "What's wrong? Why are you home so early? I thought you all were going out?"

Nothin'. I couldn't say a word. All I could do was stand frozen.

Ms. Glo walked over to me and wrapped her arms around me. I wanted to shake the pain off. I couldn't. All I could do was bury my head in her bosom and cry.

After a few minutes of sobbing and soaking Ms. Glo's blouse, we sat down on the couch and she said, "Now tell me what happened."

"You really want to know?"

"Yes, I do, so we can talk about it."

Tears continued to fall from my eyes.

Ms. Glo wiped my tears with the backs of her hands. "My dear Yvette, *shhhhh*, don't cry. I promise you, whatever it is, we will work through it. I promise."

"You're going to think I'm stupid. And silly."

"I will not. I will never think that. Now talk to me."

"I just broke up with Brooklyn."

"Why?" she asked, sounding sincere and wiping more of my tears. "Do you want to tell me what happened?"

"He got his ex-girlfriend, Alesha, pregnant."

"Oh, wow."

"And I just feel so dumb. I should've known better than to fall in love."

"You're not dumb." She placed her hand under my chin and lifted my face to meet hers. "Do you hear me?"

I shuddered, but couldn't answer.

She continued. "Love is a beautiful thing. And you're young, Yvette. There will be lots of boys and lots of chances to be in love again."

"I'm never falling in love."

"You're right; you won't. And not because you will never love again but because, in this family, we don't fall in love, we rise in it. Now you dry your eyes and stop being so down on yourself. You are the prize, you hear me? You are beautiful, smart, and any young man is lucky to have you. And I know it hurts now, but I promise you it won't hurt forever. One day you'll look up, and I'll be sittin' real pretty at your wedding, telling everyone, That's my dear Yvette!"

Through the tears somehow a laugh managed to slip out

Ms. Glo hugged me once more, then said, "Now come on in this kitchen and let me fix you some pancakes."

Dear God, I don't want a thing to eat. All I want to do is curl up in my bed and cry for the rest of the night.

"And I don't wanna hear that you don't feel like eating. 'Cause you and I both know that my pancakes always make everything better."

32

Caught Up in the Rapture

After seeing Brooklyn in homeroom, I knew I wouldn't be able to make it through the whole day.

I was here, but not here.

I'd already sat through algebra, English III, and American history. My stomach was in knots. I kept hearing Alesha's voice in my head, and no matter how I tried to brush it off, I couldn't. I should have been on my way to Earth science for a test, before lunch, but this was where I got off.

I've been here since 7:35 a.m., and I couldn't take another moment. There was no way I was going to lunch and have to see Brooklyn again.

So while e'rybody was headed to their next class, I walked in the opposite direction. After walkin' down two long halls and rounding two corners, I finally found a side door, where I could ease out in peace. I placed my hand on the silver knob and twisted it.

"Yvette."

Shit. Mrs. Brown. Where did she come from? Run! Don't look back! Just go!

"Classes are not out there." She placed her hand over mine and peeked around the side of my face.

I looked down at the gray-and-black tiled floor, then swept my eyes up and into her face. "Mrs. Brown, I like you and all. I do. But I really have to go."

"Go where?"

"Home."

"Why?" She wrinkled her forehead.

'Cause I need some air to breathe. Now stop sweatin' me. "I, *umm*, I need to know how my baby's doin'. She wasn't feeling too well this morning," I lied. "I'm worried, and I just need to see her."

"You can see her after school. And you don't need to leave the building to find out how she's doing. You can come into my office and use the phone."

I huffed and nervously tapped my foot. "I need to see her though."

"You'll see her when the school day is done and you go home."

She was passin' me off. "I can't wait that long."

"School is over in three hours."

"Three hours is too long."

"So you're willing to get in trouble." She pointed to the cameras that I had totally missed, hanging above the door. "When all you have left in your school day is three hours? Does that sound like a wise decision?"

How did I miss those cameras?! Ugh! "I'm not tryin' to throw e'rything away, but this morning she was really sick, and then there was this time she almost choked to death on a penny . . . and I'm worried."

"Okay. I understand that." Mrs. Brown grabbed my hand and intertwined our fingers. "So come with me to my office so you can call home, ease your mind, and get back to class." She practically pulled me down the hallway and into her office, where she closed the door. She pointed to the chair next to her desk. "Have a seat." She handed me the phone. "Go ahead; call home."

I dialed Ms. Glo's number and she answered on the first ring. "Hello?"

"Hey, Ms. Glo, it's Yvette."

"Is everything okay?" she asked.

"Yeah, it's all right."

"Then why aren't you in class?"

"Mrs. Brown let me use her phone to check on Kamari."

"You hear all that noise." Ms. Glo paused and I tuned into her background where I could hear children laughin' and playin'. She continued. "That's Kamari. She's been playing since they came this morning. Doing the same thing she does every day. So don't you worry about Kamari. She's fine."

"Oh...okay..."

"Listen, I know today might feel tough, but like I told you last night, you will get through it. I promise you will. Now get back to class and we'll see you when you get home. Okay?"

"Okay."

Click.

I held the receiver in my hand until a loud busy signal invaded the silence. I looked over at Mrs. Brown and handed her the phone. "I still gotta get outta here."

"Why? Did Ms. Glo say that something was wrong? Let

me call her back." Mrs. Brown picked up the phone to re-dial the number.

"No," I said, "Ms. Glo said that everything was fine."

Mrs. Brown hung up the phone. "Then what's the problem?"

"I just need to go."

"Why?"

I was seconds from losing it. I swallowed. "Mrs. Brown..."

"I'm listening."

"I just don't know if this is the place for me."

She looked concerned. "What do you mean? You're doing excellent work. Your teachers have glowing reports about you. I thought you were giving everything a chance. What are you scared of?"

I huffed. "Scared? I'm not scared of anything."

"Everybody's scared of something."

"I'm not e'rybody." This trick was buggin' and I was sick of her always in my business. I stood up. "Okay, I need to get to class."

"So now you're in a rush to get to class?" she asked. "Have a seat, Yvette."

Reluctantly, I did as she asked. The chair's cushion whooshed as I flopped down and flung one thigh over the other. I swung my foot. "Please don't start in on me. Not today. I'm just goin' through some things, and I don't want to talk about it. It's not that deep, and I'm not in the mood for you to tell me about me."

"I don't always have to do that, Yvette. I'm a great lis-tener too."

"I don't want to talk about it." I paused. I could feel dumb and stupid tears inching into my eyes. Ugh! I hated to cry. Hated. It.

Mrs. Brown reached for my hand and clasped it between hers. It took all my power not to snatch it away. She said, "I promise you, you will be just fine."

Silence.

She continued, "I know you're scared and you may even feel like you're out here by yourself."

"I am by myself."

She softly squeezed my hand. "You're not."

"Yes, I am. I'm not like these other kids here. My life is different."

"Everybody's life is different. Yvette, listen to me. You are a bright girl. All you need is someone who believes in you. And I believe in you."

"Yeah," I said sarcastically as the late bell rang. "I believe in me, too, so can I go now?"

"Yeah, go on. Just know that I'm here if you need me."

"I know, Mrs. Brown. I know."

33

No Scrubs

"Earth to Yvette." Reesie, who sat across from me at the lunch table, snapped her fingers directly in my face. "Hello, hello, helllooooooo. Earth. To. Yvettttttttttte."

Before I could ask her what planet did she think I was on, Ebony, who sat next to Reesie, said, "For real, though, Yvette. Like what's the scenario, yo? 'Cause obviously you got a deally-o." She smiled. "That's a hot line right? That's the hook for my baby, Black Conscious's, upcoming single."

"Yeah, that was dope." Reesie grinned. "And when are you goin' to hook me up with one of his friends? See how you do, Ebony. You wanna be the only one with the fly boo-juice." She looked back over at me. "Now, Yvette, I asked you a question, what's wrong? 'Cause you actin' like you got one foot in the casket and the other in the electric chair."

I was so over these two.

And, no, they hadn't done anything to me. I just didn't

know how to tell them, or even if I wanted to tell them, that Alesha was pregnant by my boyfriend.

"It's no scenario and no deally-o. I'm fine," I said, forcing myself to take a small bite of my turkey and cheese sandwich that I had no appetite for and really wanted to spit out. But I didn't. Instead, I swallowed it and it hit the bottom of my stomach like a stone.

"We know something is wrong with you," Reesie said, "I don't know why you're frontin'."

"Would y'all drop it!" I said.

I knew Reesie was only concerned about me and I shouldn't have snapped at her, but damn, she didn't know when to bug off. All I needed was a minute to collect myself and get my feelings in check. Especially since I was the one in the crew who never acted sad or bothered by anything.

I had to be the tough one. 'Cause that was the role I liked. The queen of no-sweat. The one who always gave the bomb girlfriend advice about life. The one to always tell my crew, when a boo hurt their feelings, that boys came a dime a dozen. And the secret to surviving love was to dump them before they could dump you.

"Look, Reesie, I'm sorry for snappin'. But I'm fine. Seriously, I am." I tried to smile but failed.

Reesie wasn't buying it. "Lies and deceit." She slammed her hands on the table. "We're your friends and we know you're lyin'. The question is, why?"

Ebony said, "You look like you're two seconds from crying."

I was.

Tasha popped her lips and blurted, "She and Brooklyn broke up."

"What?!" Ebony and Reesie said simultaneously.

I gasped and said, pissed off, "Tasha, you promised you wouldn't say anything!"

Tasha spat, "I couldn't hold it in another minute. Plus, I'm tired of you being all quiet and depressed. I want the old Yvette back."

"So why did y'all break up?" Ebony said.

"I wanna know that too," Reesie demanded, "'cause I'm not accepting you two breaking up. After Jerelle, you and Brooklyn restored my faith in black love. Y'all were my brown sugar. Sweet molasses in the summer time. Oh hell, no! This ain't about to go down."

"Did he cheat on you or something?" Ebony asked.

"Ebony," Reesie said, "I was thinking the same thing, 'cause what else could it be?"

Tasha snapped, runnin' her mouth like I wasn't even sittin' there. "The problem is your girl Alesha."

Reesie cocked her neck to the left and parked it there. "Say what? Hold up; back up and rewind. See, this is how rumors get started. For one, she is not my girl. Y'all"—she pointed at the three of us—"are my girls. Me and Alesha are just cool. I thought her brother was cute, and I was using her to get close to him. That's it. Plus, y'all know I'm friendly with everybody. Watch this." She turned around and waved at the students who sat at the table behind us. "Hey, Reesie!" they called out and waved back.

Reesie returned her attention to us. "I call them the United Nations. 'Cause one of them is Chinese, one Dominican, and the girl on the end is albino. I'm nice to everybody, but that don't make them my friends. And that includes Alesha. Now what that ho do?"

"Well," I said, finally speakin' up. "She's pregnant. By Brooklyn."

Reesie looked taken aback. "Pregnant? When did that happen and by whom again?"

"Brooklyn," Tasha said.

"What? Are you sure?" Ebony asked.

Reesie snapped, "That trick is lyin'! She just asked me for a tampon in the bathroom this morning. So did she get pregnant in the last five minutes?"

Tampon? "She told Brooklyn she was three months pregnant," I said.

"Lies and deceit. Ain't no way!" Reesie insisted. "So is Brooklyn saying he was cheating on you with Alesha? Oh, I will cuss both of their raggedy behinds out!"

I said, "No, he claims he was with her close to four months ago and that if she is pregnant, he don't think it's his. Whatever."

Reesie said, "Don't believe the hype. She talkin' all that jazz because she's jealous of you and mad because Brooklyn loves you. I wouldn't let her have my man." Reesie shook her head and hopped out of her seat. "So you need to get up out of that funk, come with me over there, and let's go check this ho about your man! Hell with that sad woe-is-me crap. Screw that!"

"Reesie, wait!" I said. "They not even worth it. Let it go!"

"Girl, please. I'ma go handle that!" She stormed over to the table where Brooklyn sat and Alesha stood beside him looking mad, with her arms folded over her chest. "Excuse you," Reesie looked over at Brooklyn. "You know it's about to go down, right?"

"Reesie!" I said, as me, Tasha, and Ebony all hopped out

of our seats and rushed over to her side. "Chill. I don't even care."

"Oh, you care," Reesie stated. "And I don't like liars. Plus, this is more about me than you. I need my faith in black love restored." She looked over at Alesha. "Now, back to you, Miss Stank-A-Dank. I heard you're supposed to be pregnant."

"Why are you in my business?" Alesha snapped.

"When you messed with my girl, you made it *my* business! Now I wanna know how are you pregnant when I just gave you a tampon in the bathroom this morning?"

"This morning?" Brooklyn said, taken aback.

Alesha's mouth dropped open; then she said, "I don't have to explain nothin' to you. You're not my man."

Brooklyn snapped, "I'm not your man either, so don't even come over here with that! So just like I thought, you lied."

"I don't have to lie about bein' pregnant!" Alesha screamed. "I took the test and I haven't had my period in a month. She didn't give me no tampon!"

"A month?" Brooklyn frowned. "You told me three months!"

"I said three weeks!"

"You are a three-weeks lie!" Reesie said. "'Cause your period was on this morning!"

"Yo, I can't believe you!" Brooklyn spat. "I should've known better than to even think for a moment that you were tellin' the truth. Get away from me!"

Alesha looked at Reesie and just as she charged toward her, the security guard stepped in.

"What's goin' on over here?! Break it up!"

"You better not let me catch you!" Alesha screamed at Reesie.

Ebony cocked her neck. "Trick, we'll be out after school waitin' on you. If you want it, come get it."

Reesie looked at me. "Told you she was lyin'. Lyin' on black love, you ain't gon' have no good luck." She shook her head. "Now go get your man, kiss, and make up."

I glanced over at Brooklyn and for a moment I considered doin' exactly what Reesie had said. Then I remembered that this wasn't a romance novel; this was life, and life ain't work that way. And as far as renewing my boo-vows with Brooklyn, I wasn't up for it.

The bell rang.

I turned away from Brooklyn and said to Reesie, "I gotta get to class. I don't wanna be late."

34

It's Love

Summer: A month later

It was a sweltering ninety degrees in July. Me, Tasha, and Kamari had just come back from the park, when Tasha stopped in the middle of our block and said, "Wait a minute; is that Brooklyn?"

She peered at Ms. Glo's porch, then said, "Yeah, baby. *Umm-hmm.* That's him sitting on the bottom step, and from the look on his face, he's been sitting there for a minute. Wait until I tell Reesie and Ebony this."

"You tell everything." I sucked my teeth.

"Whatever," she said.

"Guess Brooklyn doesn't take no easily," I said, more to myself than to Tasha.

"Guess not," Tasha said. "You'd better go and get your man. He's sitting there looking all hungry for you. If I was you, I'd probably run to him and jump in his arms."

"Thank goodness I'm not you. And he is not my man; you know that," I said, holding Kamari's hand.

"Tell him that. Come on, Kamari. I'll race you inside to get some of Aunty Glo's homemade ice cream."

"Ice cream!" Kamari screamed, as she and Tasha took off down the street and up the porch steps. They waved at Brooklyn before going inside and closing the door behind them.

Don't smile.

And don't trip.

Just ask him. "Is your phone broken or somethin'?" I said, and pointed. "There is a pay phone down the street, unless you didn't have a quarter. But, *umm*, either way, you could've called me before you staked out my porch and posted up. That's a bit much, don't you think?"

"You can chill with all that mouth. You know I've called you, over and over again. Nobody answers and if they do, you tell Tasha or Ms. Glo to tell me you'll call me back, and you never do. I'm tired of that."

"Then you should stop calling. Step off."

"You really want me to step off?"

"You can do what you wanna do. I'm just sayin', if your feet feel the need to leave, I'm not one for stopping you."

He squinted. "Why are you acting so cold and nasty to me, Bricks?"

I blinked and shoved a hand up my hip. "Oh, now it's Bricks."

"I always call you Bricks."

"You didn't the night your baby mama stepped up on the scene. I was Yvette that night."

"She's not my baby mama. And you know I didn't mean to hurt you."

"Whether you meant it or not, you did."

"Now what?"

"Now nothing. You lied to me. Tried to twist things around and make me seem like the problem. Maybe I didn't handle it the best way, but I was trying to get my thoughts straight. Not break us up." I flicked my wrist. "Whatever. It's cool. I could care less. We tried love; it didn't work. It never works, and I just added you to the dime-a-dozen bullshitters who have passed through my life."

Brooklyn paused. I could tell that my comments struck him right where I wanted them to, in the heart.

"All of this behind one mistake. So everything else we shared no longer matters? So Alesha is getting what she wanted anyway," he said.

Silence.

He continued. "Answer me. So you're letting Alesha win? You throwing in the towel now."

"Reverse psych is not about to work on me."

He stood up and walked over to me. "*You know* I didn't mean to hurt you. *You know* I never meant to make you question my love for you."

He pressed his forehead against mine and being so close to him melted my resistance. I hated that he smelled so good and looked so sweet. He'd cut his braids and had a fresh fade with waves, baggy blue jeans, and a plain white tee. I just wanted to rub my hands over his head and surf my fingers through his waves.

I took a step back. Brooklyn grabbed my hand and pulled me toward him.

Push him away.

No, stay.

"Stop running from me," he said.

"I'm not." I fidgeted.

Brooklyn continued. "I know I should have said something to you when Alesha first told me she was pregnant. But I didn't know how to, and I didn't want to lose you."

"You should've just told me the truth. You think I wanted to break up with you? You think I wanted to end things between us?! No! But I had to."

"We can go back and forth all day about what should and should not have happened. All I know is that I want you back. You have to give me a second chance."

"I don't know if I can do that." I dropped my gaze to the ground and then looked back up at him.

"Well, then, you're going to have to tell me how to handle this 'cause I'm not ready to let you go. And if that means I have to come here every day, all summer long, until you take me back, then that's what I'ma have to do."

I shook my head. "So are those your plans for the summer, to be a stalker?"

"I'd rather be your man, but, hey, I have to start somewhere."

I hated that he made me laugh.

"There it goes." He lifted my chin. "There it is. My Bricks. Come on, baby." He brushed his lips against mine. "You gotta give me another chance." He kissed me. "Don't make me beg."

"I'm not trying to make you beg, but I've never been good at giving out second chances."

"Bricks, life itself is a chance. You can't play it safe forever. Sometimes you gotta close your eyes and leap."

"I don't know, Brooklyn."

"What don't you know? You know that I love you. I know that you love me. That's all that matters."

I looked into Brooklyn's brown eyes, and I knew without a doubt that he loved me. "No matter how hard it is, you have to always tell me the truth," I said.

"I will."

"No more secrets."

"No more," he agreed. "I love you, Bricks."

"I love you too, Brooklyn." And at that moment, I closed my eyes and let my heart jump off the cliff.

35

Ride the Rhythm

September

I'd had the bomb summer. Chillin' with my baby, my boo, and my crew. Today was the first day of school, my senior year. I couldn't believe it. I never thought I'd ever go back to high school, let alone be a high school senior.

Of course, the guidance counselor's office was my first trip of the morning.

"Hey, Mrs. Brown," I said as I walked into her office and sat down in the chair next to her desk. "How are you? How was your summer?"

Mrs. Brown's smile was a mile wide. Her southern drawl was in full effect as she said, "Well looka here! Is this my girl, Yvette? You'd better get your hind parts up and give me a hug!"

I stood up and Mrs. Brown welcomed me into her warm embrace. "Look at you! You're glowing, beaming, and smiling. This is not even close to what you were doing when you walked in here last year this time."

I chuckled. "I know. I guess you were right. I needed to give this place a chance."

"And give yourself a chance. Remember when you asked me what would happen if you failed?" She smiled, looking me over.

"And you asked me what happened if I succeeded."

"And look at you now." She paused and her eyes continued to pleasantly drink me in. "Sit down. Fill me in on everything. I want to hear all about your summer and everything that going on."

I sat down and said, "I had a great summer. Went to the beach a hundred times, hung out with my friends, hung out with Kamari. Ms. Glo took me, Tasha, and Kamari to Myrtle Beach for a vacation. We also went to Ocean City, Maryland. She said that next summer we'll go to the Bahamas or Jamaica. My eyes popped wide open. Who would've thought I'd ever be in the Bahamas or Jamaica? Or any place other than Newark. There was a time I ain't never think I'd leave my county."

"And here you are," Mrs. Brown said. "Out of the city, out of the county, out of the state."

"And next stop is out of the country," I said.

"That's right!"

"Yeah," I nodded. "I'm feelin' that."

"So I take it you like it here?" She chuckled.

"Yeah, I do. I didn't think I would, but now I feel like this is my home."

"Norfolk feels like home?"

"Yes. Norfolk and, most of all, Ms. Glo's. She and

Tasha are like my family. I feel like they got my back, you know."

She nodded. "Yes, I know. That's important, to feel like someone has your back and you're not alone. It allows you to trust people again. You needed that."

"Yeah, I did. And I still do."

"How's Kamari? Does she like it here?" Mrs. Brown asked.

"Oh, God, yes! Kamari loves it here. She loves Ms. Glo and Ms. Glo loves her. Ms. Glo told me last night that she thinks she spoils Kamari too much. Do you know she's already started shopping for Kamari's birthday party? She'll be three next month."

"Well, happy early birthday to Miss Kamari! I'm sure the party will be wonderful."

"Ms. Glo is a beautiful person," I said.

"Yes, she is, and I'm sure you're thankful for her."

"I am."

"Do you think she spoils Kamari too much?"

I shrugged. "Maybe. Yeah, I think so. But I guess that's what grandmothers do. I don't really know. The one person I called *grandmother* was a nasty and miserable old skeezer." I realized what I'd said to Mrs. Brown, so I spat out, "I didn't mean that; I meant heifer. No, I meant, ho. No, lady. I meant a miserable old lady."

"I'll bet that's exactly what you mean." Mrs. Brown smirked.

I continued. "So, all that to say that I have no idea how a grandmother is supposed to act, but it seems like Ms. Glo might be on to something."

"Yeah, Yvette, I'd have to agree. Maybe Ms. Glo is on to something," Mrs. Brown said. "Tell me, though, after living with Ms. Glo why do you think your grandmother might have been so mean?"

"Nana was mean because it was Tuesday. Because the wind was blowing, and the leaves were on the ground."

"You really believe that?" Mrs. Brown asked.

I sat quietly and thought about what Mrs. Brown was really asking me. It crossed my mind how mean and nasty I was when I first came here. "Well, maybe she's never had anyone be nice to her. Anyone to show her how to be kind. Maybe she's mean because she's hurt."

Mrs. Brown smiled. "Yvette, yes! Now what about your mother? Have you heard anything about her or her whereabouts?"

"No. And I guess next up is the milk carton or the newspaper in the Lost-and-Found Junkie section."

"Don't call your mother names."

"The truth could never be a name, but, okay, Mrs. Brown, I won't call her a junkie. Although that's what she is. You know, I used to think about her all the time; now I don't even care."

"You don't care?" Mrs. Brown arched a brow.

"Well, I care, but I try not to focus on her. I will never understand my mother and how she could just leave us any and everywhere and never look back. How could a mother do that to her children?"

"Maybe, like your nana who may not have had anybody to be kind to her, perhaps your mother didn't have anyone who wanted her around, so she took flight before she got hurt."

"By her kids? We loved her. I don't think so. I think she was just chasing a high, and that was more important than we were."

"I think, in time, you will see that your mother loves you the best way that she can."

"Yeah, I'ma need a whole lot of time to believe that. You know what, Mrs. Brown?"

"What's that?"

"You stay goin' deep."

"Well, that's what I'm here for—to make you think."

"I do think about my little brothers and sister. I wonder how they're doing."

"Maybe you should write them a letter," Mrs. Brown suggested.

"Yeah, maybe."

Mrs. Brown continued. "Now tell me this, how do you feel about your life back in Jersey? Do you want to return?"

"I don't think so. I just want to stay here. Not move back."

"Okay. And one more thing before the bell rings, how's your love life?"

"Mrs. Brown." I blushed, suddenly feeling shy.

"Well, I know you have one. A pretty girl like you, I can only imagine how boys and their hormones are lined up. I want you to know that boys are okay, but you have time for that. Plenty of time. I want you to stay focused on school. And at the same time, if you have a boyfriend, make sure you two share similar goals. And that he wants to be something in life."

"We do," I said. "He wants to be a lawyer."

"We?" Her eyes lit up. "And he wants to be an attorney. Impressive. Are you going to tell me his name?"

"Brooklyn."

"You made up."

"Yeah." I blushed.

She clapped her hands in approval. "I'm happy for you. He's a great kid. You made a wonderful choice. And I know for sure he's going to college, which leads me to you. This is your senior year; what are your plans?"

Plans? "To find a job."

"And college?"

College? "I'm not going to college."

"Why not?" She looked puzzled.

"I'm just not."

"And why not? Last year you were a straight-A student. I expect the same this year. There are a lot of great colleges around here."

"Mrs. Brown, who's going to pay for that?"

"You can get a scholarship. Where there's a will, there's a way. You just have to want it. And together, you and I can make it happen."

"Mrs. Brown, you realize that when I first came here, I didn't think I would stay the whole day in school, let alone go to college. One thing at a time here."

"And you survived your first day, and the day after that, and the day after that. You will be fine."

I paused and drifted into a thought. "You really think I could go to college?"

"I think you can do anything you set your mind to. And, yes, even go to college."

36

Back to Life

I'm closing my home...and I'm done with foster parenting. I've had enough.

That was what drop-kicked me in the chest and sailed my stomach to my feet the moment I walked through Ms. Glo's front door from school. I couldn't believe my ears.

I'd forgotten my year was up. That I'd been livin' my life on a timeline, and not a never-ending supply of days to do whatever I wanted to do, or bloom into whoever I wanted to be. I had an invisible clock attached to me. And it had stopped tickin'.

Now my life was back to bein' at e'rybody else's mercy, a screwed-up movie, directed by e'rybody else's thoughts and beliefs of what was best for me and Kamari. I knew nobody would ask me what I wanted. I also knew that if I blurted it out, especially with my social worker sittin' on the couch—pen, pad, and my life in hand—she and Ms. Glo would think I was pissed off again.

And I was.

Pissed off that I'd forgotten I ain't really live here.

This was not my home.

My family.

My crew.

My hood.

This was Oz, and Ms. Glo was the fake-ass Wiz, who'd built you up with hope, love, laughter, dreams, deep thoughts, good times, courage, and the indescribable feelin' of comin' home to somebody, besides Kamari, whose face lit up when you stepped into the room. Only for you to reach the end and find out all she really offered was a deflated balloon that led to the land of nowhere.

I was so stupid.

I let the screen door slam behind me, so they'd know I'd stepped into the living room. Janette looked over at me, her face covered in surprise. "Hello, Yvette. I didn't expect you home from school so soon."

Ms. Glo's face lit up the way it always did. "Did they let you all out early today?" she asked.

"Yeah." I hesitated. "It was a half day."

"Great." Janette smiled. "Ms. Glo was just telling me that you're doing incredibly well."

I shrugged. "I guess." I didn't know what else to say.

Ms. Glo looked at me strangely, then walked over and draped an arm over my shoulder. She said, "I was just telling Janette how much you've grown over the last year. How you are such a respectful and beautiful young lady. That anything I ask you to do, you're right there. And what a wonderful mother you are to Kamari." She squeezed me tight.

Janette grinned. "She also told me that there was a certain young man, your age, who was hanging around quite a bit."

I didn't even respond to that. 'Cause as far as I was concerned after today Brooklyn, along with e'rything else I had to leave here, no longer existed.

Heat rose up my back and made me want to shake Ms. Glo's arm off of me, but I was trying to collect myself, so that I didn't pop off, or worse, burst into tears.

"So do you want to tell me about this special young man?" Janette said, like we were on the verge of being girl-friends. Not.

"No," I said a little too fast. "I don't."

Janette squinted. "Why not?"

"Yvette," Ms. Glo said, "I apologize if you feel like I violated your privacy, but Janette was so proud of your progress and the great choices you've made, I wanted to fill her in on everything."

"Yeah, well," I stepped out of Ms. Glo's embrace. "I also heard you fill her in on how you're closing your home and you've had enough of me and my baby."

"That's not true," Ms. Glo said defensively. "Where did you get that from?"

I bit the corner of my bottom lip.

Say what you gotta say and you better not cry. Don't drop one tear. You are not weak. And somehow, some-way, you gon' handle this.

"Look, Ms. Glo. It's cool. Thank you for the last year that me and my baby have been here. Y'all was like family, but e'rybody knows that nothin' good last forever. And my time is up." I looked over at Janette. "That was the agreement, right? A year?"

Janette answered, "Well, yeah, but..."

"No need for buts; it's cool. Did you really think that I thought I'd be here forever? What'd you think, I forgot? Psst, please. I was just waiting out my time, chillin like a villain."

"Yvette," Ms. Glo said, "that is not how you feel, and you know it."

I cocked my neck to the side. "Now you're telling me how I feel? Is that your new business? You've gone from taking kids into your home, having them love you like a mother, to now being a mind reader?" I clapped my hands. "Good job, Ms. Glo." I looked back over at Janette. Tears pounded against the backs of my eyes.

Don't cry.

My eyes burned and tears crept around the brim. I was doin' my all to push them back, but failed.

I wiped my moist cheeks with the backs of my hands. "Look, I'm not some weak little girl. I got this. Okay. I knew what time it was when I got here. So all I wanna know is where am I goin' from here? Can I do independent living or something?"

"Independent living?" Janette looked taken aback. "You want to live alone? You're a teenager. Don't you want a family?"

"Kamari is all the family I need. I don't need nobody else. Not Ms. Glo, not Tasha, and damn sure not my mother who's been swallowed up by the street. Me, myself, and I, and Kamari, we good."

Janette shook her head. "No. I don't think independent living is what's best for you or Kamari. You need a family."

"I don't need nobody!" I screamed. "I'm so tired of e'rybody tellin' me what they think is best for me! Nobody cares about that. Nobody. All of my life I've lived from pil-

lar to post. Had to beg, borrow, and steal love from whoever my mother left me with. I'm tired of that. I'm tired of
loving people who don't love me back. That's why I had
my baby, so I would know that no matter what, somebody
was there for me. There to always love me. So please, let
me, for once, make my own decisions."

"Yvette," Ms. Glo said, "listen you misunderstood..."

"No, when I walked in the door, I understood perfectly
well and I heard all I needed to hear. You're closing your
home. You can't do it anymore. The year is up. And you're
right, my time's up." I wiped more tears. "All I'm asking,
Janette, is that you please don't place me with more people. I just wanna be by myself."

"So you didn't like it here?" Janette asked.

"I loved it here!" I said too fast, when I should've said
the opposite. "This was my home. And yeah, okay, okay, I
know I said I didn't forget that my time here was limited,
but I did. I forgot that this was a plea bargain sentence. I
love Ms. Glo and I love Tasha. They're like my family. But
I've had enough of families who you love but don't love
you back."

Ms. Glo grabbed both of my hands. "Listen..."

"Ms. Glo..."

"Be quiet."

"Ms. Glo..."

"Be. Quiet. And listen to me. When you walked in the
door I was telling Janette that I no longer wanted to be a
professional parent. That I loved you and Tasha, and Kamari like my own. And I couldn't imagine you three being
anywhere else but with me. That's why I said I was closing
my home. Not because the year is up and I want to put
you out, but because I want to keep you. Whether you be-

lieve it or not, you're my family too. So no, I don't want you to leave. I want you to stay. But if you want to leave, I'll understand."

I wanted to say something. I just didn't know what.

"Yvette," Janette said, "as you know your mother has been missing for some time now, and the state would like to move forward with finding you an adoptive family."

I sucked my teeth. This chick just went from bad to worse. I dropped Ms. Glo's hands and took a step back. "Adoption, at my age? Yeah, okay. Like somebody really wanna adopt a teen with a baby."

"I would like to adopt you," Ms. Glo said. "If you'll allow me to. I know I'll never be your biological mother, and I don't ever want to take her place. I just want you and Tasha and Kamari to officially be a part of my family. So what do you think about that?"

Silence.

Complete silence.

What do you think about that?

I ain't know what to think about that. About this. It all felt too good. Too real. Too possible. Too much like a fairy-tale.

This wasn't Wonderland.

But it was everything I'd ever wanted.

And the complete opposite of what I thought I'd ever get. No Nana. Munch. Jail. Loosies. Forties. Flip.

No fear.

Just this: Somebody who loved me and wanted me around.

But did I deserve this? Was I worthy? I was a street kid, who came here with nothin' but an attitude, a court ordered sentence, and a toddler in tow.

I wasn't Perfect Patty.

I was Yvette, with a baby.

I looked over at Ms. Glo, who Kamari had just walked over to with her arms out. Ms. Glo picked her up and Kamari laid her head on Ms. Glo's shoulder.

This was my family.

I walked over to Ms. Glo, hugged her and said, "I think I'd like that."

Don't miss the first book in the Throwback Diaries series
Down by Law

Available wherever books are sold

1

The Message

All I could do was get off the ground and run.
No lookin' back.

No time to hook off on nobody.

Just zoom through the streets of Newark until I reached the corner of Muhammad Ali and Martin Luther King Boulevard and made a mad dash for Douglas Gardens. Better known as *Da Bricks*. Twenty L-shaped, seven-story buildings that took up four blocks, connected by a courtyard. To the right was a basketball hoop. No net. Just a rim. To the left was a row of ten rusted clotheslines, where the only thing that hung safely was a beat-up pair of white Converses.

There were begging-behind crackheads er'where, scratching they necks, carrying they snotty-nose babies on they hips. And dope fiends who stood up, nodded out, but never fell down.

There were some people leavin' out for work. And some

just coming in; rushing straight from the bus stop to they apartment. Never speaking to nobody. Never looking no other way but straight. Never coming back outside until the next day.

Old ladies hung out the window and cussed out anybody making noise.

Winos sat on the stoops and complained about yesterday, every day.

Somebody's boom box echoed through the air. And another somebody was spittin' rhymes.

Kids raced behind the ice cream truck like roaches who'd seen the light.

Fresh ballers had a pot of money at their side while they rolled dice.

B-Boys break danced, making the cardboard come alive.

Then there was me. Twelve-year-old Isis. Five feet even. Short arms. Short legs. Skin the color of honey. A too-big booty bouncing. And size six feet zippin' er'thing, as I burst into building one-seventy-two, rushed up the pissy stairway, and swore that once I got inside, to apartment three-twenty-five, I was never gon' come back out. Ever.

"What da hell wrong witchu?" Daddy stood up and slammed both hands on the kitchen table as I clung to his waist and buried my head into his side. My mother, Queenie, and brother, Face, did they best to stop the guns, blades, and bricks of rock that lay on the glass table top from sliding to the floor.

"Isis. You hear me?" Daddy lifted my chin.

I didn't answer him. Instead, I wiped snot with the back of my bruised and trembling hand.

Queenie frowned. Shoved a hand up on her hip. "Ain't

nuttin' wrong wit' this lil high yellow heifer." She snorted and popped her full lips. "'Cept she selfish as the day is long. Mannish. Spoiled. And she stay lookin' for a reason to tear up our groove and bust up our party. But I tell ya what: Had my rock hit the floor, or one of them guns went off, you was gon' have a reason for dem tears. Now tell us what happened to you!"

"Relax, Queenie," Daddy said sternly. "Now, baby girl—"

"Baby?" Queenie sucked her teeth. "This strumpet ain't no baby. When I was her age, I was ripe, ready, and on my own. Baby? Puhlease. Ain't no dang babies around here. Now, Isis, you heard what I said—"

"Pop! Queenie!" My fourteen-year-old brother, Montez—who we called Schooly 'cause Queenie said it didn't matter that he was a touch of retarded, he was still the smartest black man she knew—bolted into the room. "Yvette is at the door crying and saying some chicks jumped and jacked Isis for her Shell Toe Adidas and her dookie chain."

"And my neon jelly bracelets!" Yvette's quivering voice squeaked in from the hallway.

I could feel all eyes land on me.

Before I could decide what to do, Face stuffed a nine at his side.

"Sit down," Queenie said. "And put that gun back on the table."

"But Queenie," he pressed.

"What did I say?!"

He put the gun back and Queenie walked over to me. She slung me around, and my wet lashes kissed the base of her brown neck.

"You let some hos do what to you?" She shoved me into the corner and sank her elbow into my throat, pinning me against the wall. The heels of my bare feet was in the air and the tips of my toes just swept the floor.

My heart raced.

Rocks filled my mouth.

I couldn't breathe.

I couldn't think.

All I could do was suck up snot and do my best to not to choke on it.

Queenie pressed her elbow deeper into my throat, causin' me to gag. "Look at me when I'm talkin' to you! You out there in the street lettin' some hos disrespect you?"

I lifted my gaze to meet hers and spotted a gleamin' blade in her right hand. My eyes sprang wide and drops of piss drowned the seat of my panties.

I froze.

She leaned into my ear. *"I asked you a question."*

Silence.

"Answer me!"

"I can't...breathe...."

She eased the pressure of her elbow a little, just enough so that I could speak but not too much where I could move. I licked the salty tears that ran over my lips. My stomach bubbled and I knew at any moment Queenie's elbow would be speckled orange.

I hesitated. "They-they-they-they-they...snuck us. We was mindin' our business and they stole on me. All me and Yvette was doin' was walkin' down the street and some chicks came outta nowhere. I swear to *God*, Queenie, I didn't see 'em comin'."

"Who was it?"

My eyes shifted from hers to the floor. "I don't know." I shrugged. Then looked back at her.

Queenie eyed me from my torn neon-pink and stretched-neck T-shirt, to my skin-tight Jordache jeans. Her thin neck turned into a road map of thumping veins and her glare burned its way through me.

I chewed the corner of my bottom lip.

Queenie was going to kill me. Question was: when?

I glanced over at a boney and freckle-faced Schooly, whose sunken chestnut eyes revealed that he was petrified. He was nothing like our eighteen-year-old brother, Ezekiel Jr., who up until he saw the movie *Scarface* we'd called Lil Zeke. Now we had to call him Face.

Face would try anything once, including runnin' up on Queenie. But Schooly...Schooly was slow. A straight pussy. Always went to school. Never smoked weed. Never did no licks wit' us. Never got in no trouble. Never talked back. And with his twisted left leg that dragged, there was no way he was gon' leap over here and save me.

I looked toward the doorway. A teary-eyed Yvette stood peekin' into the kitchen. Another useless one.

Queenie snatched my face around. "As much as you stay fightin' in school and I have to cuss the teacher out. And as much as you 'round here tryna fly kick Face in the chest and he makes two of you, ain't no way you got robbed. You musta gave it to 'em."

"Nah-uhn," I spat, shaking my head. More tears filled my eyes. "They jacked us. At the store. Soon's we walked out the door. Knocked Yvette out cold. Slapped me to the ground and straight jacked me for er'thang. I was looking fresh to def too."

I scanned Queenie's eyes. They narrowed to icy green

slits. She pointed the tip of the blade lightly into my jugular and I held my breath.

Hot specks of spit checkered my face as she said, "One thing I can't stand is somebody tryna play me. You must want me to slice your lil lyin' throat open and whip yo' fresh lil—"

"Okay. Okay. Just pleeeeeeeeease don't kill me. Pleeeeeeeease. Queenie. See ummm, what had happen was, ummm—I was in a break-dancin' battle—" My heart raced and my body dripped with sweat. Queenie hated break dancin'. "And the prize was a Doug E. Fresh cassette tape." And she hated cassette tapes. She was stuck on forty-fives and eight-tracks. "But I wanted that tape baaaaad. So I killed it on the cardboard. And this girl Aiesha and her crew got mad 'cause I won."

"And . . ."

"I called 'em fake break-dancin' hos. I gave 'em the middle finger and told 'em to take they ugly behinds home. But. That didn't give 'em no reason to jack us!"

"And they was bigger than us!" Yvette tossed in. *"Waaaaaaay* bigger than us!"

"I know you ain't care about no size?!" Queenie snapped, grimacin' at me. "I know you ain't stand out there and let some ho beat you down 'cause she was big?!"

"No!" I practically shook my head off. "Size don't matter to me. 'Cause I woulda left they lungs on the sidewalk. But. It was four of them and only two of us. It wasn't a fair one, Queenie." Fresh tears sprang from my eyes. "Now I don't have nothin'. Not my favorite sneakers. Not my chain. And not my tape. How I'ma be fly *and* jacked? That's bad. Real bad. Hella bad."

"And where they jack you at?"

I sucked in a breath. Slowly eased it outta the side of my mouth. "We dipped off."

"Where?"

I hesitated. "Umm...we was in Weequahic—" Before I could finish, Queenie slapped me so hard that my neck whipped to the left and a gush of spit kicked its way through my lips.

She'd told me a million times to stay outta the park. That too many girls was raped and left floatin' face down in the lake. But...I was nowhere near the lake. The break-dancin' battles was always on the playground. I started to tell her that, but judging by the look on her face, I didn't think now would be a good time.

Besides, it was no secret that Queenie hated me. Before I came burstin' through her golden coochie, she'd been daddy's bottom treat, beatin' the concrete and keepin' his stable of hos tight just to prove her love. But. Once she gave birth to me, the hustle changed.

"A'ight. That's enough, Queenie," Daddy said, finally saving my life. "Get that blade outta my baby's face and don't slap her no more."

"Zeke—"

He shot her a look. The same look he'd given her the other night when he'd told her to shut up. She hadn't listened. So he'd wrapped his belt around her neck, dragged her around the room, and made her be quiet. "I *said* that's enough. Now come here, baby girl."

Queenie grabbed me by the shoulder and pushed me over to Daddy. He pulled me into his lap and wiped my face and neck with the palm of his hand. "Did you forget who you is?"

Silence.

"Answer me."

I blinked back tears and sniffed. "No. I ain't forget."

"Well, it's lookin' that way to me. You lettin' somebody punk you in the street."

"I ain't forget, Daddy."

"Then talk to me. Lay it down fo' me. Who is Isis Carter?"

I sucked up snot. "Yo' princess. Yo' baby girl, and I ain't never s'pose to be scared."

"And why is that?" Queenie interjected.

"'Cause I'm betta than that."

"And...?" Daddy pressed.

"I know my rep is er'thing. That's why I know how to shoot my own gun and fight my own fight—"

"Damn skippy." Queenie beamed.

Daddy continued, "Then you already know you gon' have to go back out there and handle this on ya own."

Silence.

"Now, go change them clothes and getchu a bat—"

"A bat? Oh, hell no. She gon' take this blade." Queenie placed the shiny metal in the palm of my hand.

My eyes bulged and my heart sank to my feet. I'd been in a whole lotta throwdowns, but this was a whole other level.

"This is war," Queenie spat. "So you may as well get your mind right. 'Cause you goin' back out there. And if you come back in here wit' out them tennis shoes, that gold chain, and that Doug E. Somebody tape, then I'ma peel the high yellah black offa you." She pointed to the pile of blades on the table. "Now try me if you want to."

Connect with U(s)

Visit us online at
KensingtonBooks.com
to read more from your favorite authors, see books
by series, view reading group guides, and more.

Join us on social media

for sneak peeks, chances to win books and prize packs,
and to share your thoughts with other readers.

facebook.com/kensingtonpublishing
twitter.com/kensingtonbooks

Tell us what you think!

To share your thoughts, submit a review,
or sign up for our eNewsletters, please visit:
KensingtonBooks.com/TellUs.